Nails

D. M. Samson has had numerous articles published and co-authored *Silent Violence*. He lives with his wife and two daughters in Germany.

First published in 2008 by David M. Samson, 20 Arundel Road, Bath, Avon BA1 6EF.

ISBN 978-0-9556796-1-2

British Library Cataloguing in Publication Data.
A catalogue record for this book is available from the British Library.

Cover design by David M. Samson.

www.davidmsamson.com

To absent friends.

Kathy Parker died 1983 (age 24)
and Tony Rosell died 1993 (age 37).

David M. Samson, April 2008

Shit, shave, shower. That was how the day started for him. Nothing out of the ordinary in that respect. But today was a Saturday and the dry, reptilian claw of a hangover gripped his brain. It squeezed internally, like something contained in a moist cloth and subject to intense heat. His very eyes protested. They seemed too big for their sockets, swollen with fluid and contrasting his parched brain. Then there was his mouth, also parched, but tasting foul, as if he had been sucking on the exhaust pipe of a car all night.

As he sat on the bog, wanting the tranquillity and sanctuary of unconsciousness, he inspected the bruise at his side. It was purple and pained.

He smiled to himself as he remembered his kick to the fucker's gut.

And with this memory other pieces of the previous evening rose up to scorch his knackered mind. Oh, how he wished for an unthinking state.

"The barrel's on tonight," said Steve.

"Aye, there's yer fuckin' dinner," said Tony, raising his pint.

They all laughed.

"You look at my woman again I'll put you in an oxygen tent!" threatened the stranger.

"Yeah, you and whose fuckin' army?" he had returned.

"Leave it out," said the stranger's girlfriend. But the stranger knew she fancied Kevin and her words pushed him over the edge.

Kevin viewed himself in the bathroom mirror.

"What a bleedin' mess," he remarked, without the

smile he had hoped for.

Perhaps he'd phone and call it off. No. He wanted to see her.

Methodically he took out his shaving implements. Every sound was as distinct as his movements were purposeful. The flush of the cistern seemed to crash forever. The rush of water in the sink seemed louder.

As he shook the can of foam with some reserve of energy he moved his head from side to side, viewing himself all the while and eventually a sardonic smile stretched his mouth-line.

"You and whose fuckin' army?" he said aloud. And he shook the can vigorously and shunned the hatchet buried deep in his head.

"Oh Kevin, Kevin, only you. Only you," she had gasped as he moved over her. Push. Push. Push.

What a love-bite she had given him! He smiled again. The lads at the garage had given him some friendly gyp over that.

Kevin checked his neck. Not a sign.

Then to counter his smile his side flared.

"Leave it out," said the stranger's girlfriend. But the stranger knew she fancied Kevin and it was enough to push him over the edge.

He shoved Kevin, who, after falling into people, spilling their drinks, had crashed into a table.

"Aye," shouted Terry.

Kevin pulled himself up. His face burnt with rage. But he knew the stranger would be ready. So he had gone real close. Stood in front of him. Using his eyes to burn holes in the bastard's face. But making no move. Fooling the fucker into thinking he was scared.

Then as Terry pushed his way through the crowded

pub, Kevin had grabbed the bloke's wrists with a vice-like grip, and like a sledgehammer he had nutted him. It was his favourite move. And with him dazed he had yanked him to him and brought his knee up into the bastard's crotch. The guy was almost on the floor when Kevin kicked him in the guts. Magic.

It all happened very fast.

Terry shouted at Kevin and got Steve and Tony to take him out.

But Terry gave the guy on the floor the greater bollocking. He was not a regular like Kevin. He was banned from the pub.

This was the second time Terry had balled Kevin out and no doubt tonight he would receive a lecture from him. Perhaps this time he would ask him to stay away for a couple of weeks. Now that would really piss him off.

After his shave he climbed into the shower and let the hot water cleanse his body. For a long while he let it run over his head. He kept his eyes open, blinking away the rivulets when they came. He hung his head in some kind of James Dean detachment. His brain was still screaming, but the patter of water on his head had a soothing distraction. Eventually the hatchet won through and he began to wash.

He dug his fingertips into the soap, hoping to scratch some of it under his bitten nails, to reach the black grease and oil that was always there.

During his soaping he came across his bruise. He ventured a depression, a little harder. Yes, he could feel it. A little harder. Yes, it hurt. It was sore.

Then suddenly, tensing his stomach muscles he made a fist and punched himself hard.

Strength, he thought to himself.

The bruise at his side began to ache.

He sang loudly, deeply. And for a moment he was Jim Morrison of The Doors.

Starkers, he left the bathroom and moved through the living room towards the kitchen.

Kevin cursed under his breath when he noticed that he'd left the stereo on all night. The ashtrays were full, sitting on the floor. Crushed cans of lager and plates covered with the specks of toast crumbs lay strewn about.

"Tip, tip, tip," he said to himself.

In the kitchen, melted yellow cheese hung in the mesh of the grill pan. Toast crumbs, coffee rings and stained teaspoons littered the work surfaces.

Kevin lifted the kettle, guessed its contents and flicked the switch. As he gathered things together, looking out on the bright day through the small kitchen window, the electric kettle hissed and then rattled and bumped. He knew that that was what came of re-boiling the same water, but he did not know why.

He returned to the lounge and put a record by Echo and the Bunnymen on the turntable. Then, beginning to feel the cool of the room because he was still in his birthday suit, he went back to the bedroom and pulled on a pair of jeans.

He looked at himself in the wardrobe's full-length mirror and pulled his stomach in, then he let it relax and watched the slight overhang.

As he puffed up his chest, raising his arms above himself and then bringing them down, all tensed and straining, the kettle switch clicked off.

Ruffling his thick black hair with a hand he went back into the living room.

This time he drew the curtains, flooding the flat, which held the stench of cigarette smoke, with the morning light. He opened a window and the room sighed.

He picked up a couple of ashtrays on his way to the kitchen, tipped their contents into the flip-top plastic bin and then turned to the cupboard. Collecting a mug and the jar of coffee he went to the sink unit drawer for a teaspoon.

"Bollocks," he said quietly, when he found their place empty.

He took one from the dirty dishes in the bowl in the sink. Under the tap-water he rubbed it with his thumb.

He was gasping for a cup of coffee, but having made it he realised it would be too hot to drink. He felt really dull.

It was then he remembered the orange juice in the fridge and he took another mug and poured himself some from the carton.

Echo and the Bunnymen were wailing away, the constant solid bass and the wandering lead guitar and vocals.

Having drunk the orange juice in one go, he suddenly did not feel like the coffee. So leaving the coffee on the sideboard he began to tidy up the living room.

Beryl moved on top of him. Riding him. He watched her, lying on his back, enjoying her joy.

He was in complete control when she came the first time. She fell upon him totally wasted, like a rag doll. He remained hard and slowly he began to move to retain his hardness. Kevin held her by the tops of her thighs as his movement became more obvious. He pushed her up and she began to ride him once again. Pain etched her face. Or was it painful joy? She was quite wet.

He felt himself swell and he lifted his buttocks off the sheets of the bed, so that she could not use her knees for support. Only him.

He feigned his coming by breathing harshly and she, obviously wanting him to come quickly, did the same. But he was a long way off and had trapped her. She had been suckered in and now her emotion took over. He would get her to come again.

She rode him wildly. And she knew she had been tricked. Or perhaps it had passed for him? No matter, she moved upon him frantically. Trying to wait for him. Not wanting to come too quickly and become unable to satisfy him. So she fought with herself.

And he knew all this and it excited him. Because he hated her. He loved their sex but that was all. His hate was why he could keep such control.

When she came the second time he came shortly afterwards, bursting painfully.

"Two times," she gasped. "That's never happened before..."

On the third ring she picked up the phone.

"Hallo Helen. It's me, Kevin."

"Oh, hallo."

"Still okay for lunchtime?"

"Yes."

"Good."

"Are you all right?"

"Yeah. Just a little hungover."

"Well, we can call it off if you want?"

"Oh no. No."

Pause.

"So," he began. "I'll see you in twenty minutes. I don't fancy driving, perhaps we can walk?"

"Yes, that'll be nice."

"Right."

"Okay, see you soon then."

"Right, cheers."

"Bye."

He put the receiver down, went over to the stereo and turned the music up again.

Call it off? Like hell.

You are

You are my field
And I have come to lie here
You are my tranquillity
And I have come to rest here

You are my sanctuary
And I have come to hide fear
You are my hope
And I have come to face fear

You are my companion
And I have come to be near
You are my love
And I have come to love here.

In the kitchen he filled the plastic bowl in the sink and opened the window. An ant raced across the sill.

Echo and the Bunnymen were sparing *the Cutter*.

He crushed it with his finger.

The breeze of the day stroked his face as he washed the dishes. But he still felt thick.

Thirteen pints at the pub, two cans of lager back here, was a little too much after a day at the garage. They'd got together straight after work and had a bite whilst drinking. He didn't want to drink a lot this lunchtime; otherwise he'd be really spaced going around the shops. He loathed Saturday shoppers at the best of times.

"Go for it, Kev."

He regarded the pint before him. A little drama never hurt anybody. He'd drink the bastard under the table any day. But down-in-one...?

And he'd lifted the pint, those years ago, and emptied it. But he had not held it down... He had not reached the loo. God, what a mess! What an embarrassment! Ha! He'd taken the guy out a few weeks later. Still...

"Right," he said to himself. "That'll do."

He wiped his hands on the tea towel and surveyed the lounge.

"Damn." He'd missed an ashtray and he'd just emptied the bowl of water.

Kevin wanted the place decent, just in case she came back. He took it to the kitchen and washed it with his fingers under warm water.

In the bedroom he gathered up the clothes, strewn or draped about and stuffed them into the wash-basket. Another trip to the launderette was well overdue. He always left it late. Once he had to wash all his underwear and the inside of his jeans had rubbed his balls sore.

It was getting on.

The record came off the turntable and a loose T-shirt was slipped over him. "Move, move, move." He clicked his fingers, checking the flat. Bedroom door closed. Windows closed. Money. Keys. Book.

"Yes, book." He picked up the book from the table and slapped it into his hand three times.

"Okay, let's hit it."

Outside, the hubbub of the day shocked him. His exuberance vanished and he again felt dull. Smile y'bastard. You can't see her like this.

A dog was barking. Some kids were screaming down

at the park. Noisy buggers.

"Sandra," he had said, wanting her attention, "will you marry me?"

"I don't know."

And he remembered a scene from earlier days.

They had been naked in the bedroom. The room was charged with emotion. He was very upset.

She said: "If this is love, then I'm very disappointed."

He cried silently and she did the same. Crying they had tenderly made love on the bed.

All this was over two years ago, he thought to himself. Why surface now? Was he going soft, again? Huh, perhaps...

As he walked down the hill, nearing the main road, passing the flats and small abused park, Lou Reed's *Femme Fatale* surfaced in perfect reproduction.

He scolded himself because it had not been like that. Sandra had been, and still was, special to him. Yes, he'd got chewed out, but it wasn't really her fault.

Nevertheless, Kevin drew strength from the lyrics and his defences came up as he crossed the busy main road. Yes, he'd be strong. After all, he felt, it was his strength that appealed to Helen. No, not his brutality, his strength, his masculinity.

He slapped the book into his thigh to the rhythm of the music in his head.

What the fuck you staring at wog? his mind asked, as the coloured approached him.

His eyes flared, but the coloured remained dead-eyed.

And he thought of Al at work. He took a lot of stick for being a nigger. But then he dished it out too. He had the respect of all of them at the garage. As long as you gauged his mood you could have a laugh. He'd beaten shit out of that new lad. Served him right too. He'd had it coming. Nobody had liked him. They were all glad when Mick sacked him.

Perhaps the wog had been watching his rhythm. Ah, he could dance. Him and the boys on the dance floor were something else.

He was always up on music. After all, the radio was on all day at work. No wonder he rarely used it in the flat!

Then he was at her door: the main door on the roadside. There was no garden. He rang her bell, one of the three that were lit up.

Ordinarily he would hear her thud thudding down the stairs, but that was because he often saw her in the evening when the traffic was not so bad. Also down the way the motorised rat-tat-tat of a pile driver intermittently drowned all sound.

Kevin's face washed over with dullness. He gripped the book slightly harder as if he felt it might fall. He had already checked his hair in the shop window next door.

The waiting began to irritate him as he looked up and down the busy road.

Maybe he ought to call it off?

Then the door opened and he jumped inside himself, but she did not notice.

"Hi," he said, forcing a smile.

She read him immediately.

"You did have a bad night."

He laughed, but not sincerely. His defences had been shaken.

"Ah well," he began, as he entered the hallway, "you've got to relax after a hard day's graft."

"Yes," she agreed, sweetly.

Now he was in disarray. Retreat or hold ground?

"How about you?" he asked, deciding to side step.

"I stayed in."

They plodded up the stairs.

"What? On a Friday night?"

"What's so special about Friday night?"

Shit, he thought. Retreat. Retreat.

"Nofing I s'pose."

Silence.

After three flights of steps they entered her flat.

"Do you want a drink or shall we get on?" she asked. He stood lamely between the entrances of her small kitchen and lounge-dining room.

"We'd better get going. Especially as we're walking."

"Okay." And she moved off into the lounge for her handbag.

He stood, with his arms hanging at his sides, looking into her immaculate flat with its hanging baskets of plants, tastefully obscure pictures in oriental water-colours and modern photographs, the upright piano, the drawing-board and easel, rows of books, Habitat sofa, two large beanbags and finally the huge cheese plant leaning out of the corner of the room.

All this made him feel threatened.

"Will I need a cardigan."

"Huh?"

She repeated the question.

"Oh, er, no. No."

"Okay, let's go." Helen smiled at him and some skin lifted from his eyes.

They made for the door.

Now was the time to establish himself. He racked his mind for something to say. Then just at the door he remembered the book.

"Oh. I brought you your book back."

"Thanks," she said, taking it from him and placing it on top of the piano. "What did you think?"

Kevin did not really want to talk about it. He had not enjoyed it at all, mainly because he had not understood it. If indeed, there had been anything to understand.

Sometime late Friday night or early Saturday morning, after the five of them had indulged a jolly post-mortem of the fight and past fights, Steve had found it on the mantle-piece.

"Mysteries, Knut Hamsun," he had said, trying to read the back cover. "Is it a thriller?"

"Naw," Kevin returned. His mates were with him tonight, so he would not put on airs. "It's about this nutter who likes to shock people."

"Any good?"

"No. Not really. I couldn't get into it."

"That architect friend of yours gave you it, didn't she?" put in Tony.

"Yeah," he replied, looking into his can, the smoke smarting his eyes.

The book of poetry, by some local struggling author, she had leant him was well hidden in his bedside cabinet. He hadn't got through it and wasn't ready to give it back. When he was, he'd make damn sure there was no chance of bumping into anybody he knew.

"I thought it quite good," he answered her. Then he felt guilt-ridden and a redness filled his neck. "But I'm not sure I understood it."

"Yes," she smiled. "He was a rather odd writer. Melancholic and philosophical."

He nodded in agreement; grateful he had got off so lightly because she had not seen his neck.

"'ave you got anywhere yet?" Tony had persisted.

"Fuck off," Kevin returned.

From the light of her flat the stairway was relatively dark.

"Y'd break y'neck on these stairs," he remarked as she closed her flat door, making it even darker.

She pressed the timed light switch.

"There we are. It's called a light switch," she said facetiously.

At that moment, with the light upon her honey-coloured hair, a winsome smile putting dimples in her cheeks, his heart leapt.

He laughed. And his head ached in protest.

They went down the stairs and out onto the brutal street. The sun brought out the drabness of the brick buildings and grey paving stones. Lorries, juggernauts, cars, all passed along this way.

For a short time they walked in silence. The noise of the traffic made conversation difficult.

Then as they turned down the alley away from the main road she spoke:

"Do you like getting drunk?"

What answer to give? Play it safe.

"Sometimes."

But it was not sufficient. Ah, throw the ball in her court.

"Don't you?" he asked.

She seemed to contemplate this for a moment as they emerged from the alleyway onto the common.

"Yes...sometimes."

He smiled and he knew that she was smiling too. He would not look at her, although she walked alongside him now. In the alley she had led.

For some reason the grassland seemed huge, the trees miles away.

Others walked across the common. A group of kids were playing football between clumps of jackets and bags. And further in the distance a party were having a barbecue. Kevin was glad their path would keep them in relative isolation.

Sandra and he had moved across such a wasteland many years ago.

"What are we going to do?" she had asked.

"Look, don't worry... But we have to get, er, rid of it."

"It," she whispered heavily.

"Look," he pleaded, distressed. "I can't think of it any other way. You mustn't either."

He put his arm around her.

"I'll stand by you," he reassured.

What a different story it would be now if they hadn't got rid of it. He would have married her. She had been keen on him then. But it hadn't happened that way...

Helen wore a plain white blouse and jeans.

"It's a lovely day," she said. Had she seen him eyeing her?

"Yes," he returned, looking at the kids way off playing football.

"It's nice taking a walk," he said.

"Yes."

"It's also nice to see you during the day... Usually when we go out it's pitch black."

"That's true. I - oh - ah -" she frantically waved a hand side to side and leant into him. It was a large bee.

"Don't hit it," he said, grabbing her shoulders and moving her away from the drunken path of the insect.

Then it was gone. He let her go and she straightened

herself.

"I hate wasps," she said, looking down her blouse.

"It was a bee."

"Same thing."

Kevin was about to pursue the matter, but then realised it would be tactless.

As they resumed their walk, he became aware that that was the first time he had touched her. He'd only taken her out three times. And on each occasion he had grown more daring in their parting kiss. She had resisted in such a way that he'd felt awkward, but not humiliated. Soon the crunch would come. But what made her tick?

"She's probably a twenty-four carat virgin," Tony had stated.

Steve had reprimanded him. "Leave it out Tone."

"What were we saying?" Helen asked.

"I can't remember."

"Neither can I."

Silence.

"Oh yes," she began, lit up by the fact that she had remembered. "Walking."

"Yes," he agreed, thinking it was a dead-end subject.

"My parents used to take my sister and myself for walks all the time. Even in winter. There are some nice walks at home."

"Naw, we never went for walks. There was nowhere to go. That's the city for you."

It had stopped raining and he walked alongside his Dad. The two of them walking into town to buy something for Mum. It would be her birthday soon.

As the street came up to the traffic lights it seemed to narrow. Far too small for the huge vehicles that used it. A lake-like puddle sat in the kerb. When they were adjacent to it, Kevin's little hand grasping his Dad's, a ten-tonner hurtled passed them towards the lights. Dad had been drenched from the waist downwards and young Kevin had been virtually soaked from head to toe.

Dad had been angry, but on seeing the state of Kevin he had decided to laugh. And they had both laughed at their misfortune.

"My Mum always has to go out on a sunny day," Helen went on. "She feels it's a waste otherwise."

A form of challenge had risen here and Kevin took it up, assuming a negative role.

"Work that's all my parents knew. So we had no time for walks."

"That's sad."

"Yeah. Mum's quite lonely now without us all...that no purpose sort of thing..."

Silence.

They had almost reached the trees at the far end of the field.

Clouds blotted out the sun now and then, making them feel quite cold.

Helen spoke again when they were on the well-trodden path between the bushes and trees. Flecks of light, like those on a pool, burnt the ever-changing, irregular-shaped gaps in the foliage.

"You didn't really like Mysteries, did you?"

"No, I guess not," he answered, somewhat ashamedly.

"I'll try and give you a more exciting one next time."

A hot flame of anger went through him, for he thought she was patronising him.

"I think books should be entertaining."

"I agree," she said, aware that she had annoyed him.

"But," she ventured, "I think they should be interesting and make you think."

Kevin was silent.

"Don't you agree."

"Yes," he replied. "But I think a story of a nobody going nowhere a bit boring."

"Fair enough."

"That's why I couldn't even finish the other one you gave me."

"Nausea, by Satre."

"Yes, that one. It was the same thing. Him and Hamsun must have been laughing all the way to the bank." He had been about to say "bleedin' bank" but he had stopped himself.

"Maybe."

This was the thing that really bugged him about her. She was caught up in the stupid psychological bullshit of life. Not living, but reading about living. He hated the assumed superiority of her. More importantly, he felt it wasn't really her. She was kidding herself. The subject would have to be dropped. He could not talk without losing his temper.

In the following silence they went across the narrow metal bridge. Two boys raced past them on bikes.

The river shimmered and sparkled; and the only noise was that of the birds and a kind of metallic rush.

Kevin struggled to shun his anger, but his mind was weak. So he sought a happy song, and the guitar and harmonica of Culture Club's *Karma Chameleon* rescued him.

His anger flew from him, banished by the bouncy tune.

"Have you ever been rowing along here?" he asked enthusiastically.

"No," she smiled.

"It's great. You get a boat down the way. Pay for the hour and off you go. Right up to the weir, if you think you can make it."

"Sounds fun."

"Better still," he continued. "I've got a mate who lives on the bank. He could get us some wine. They won't let you take it at the station. What do you think? I'll try'nd arrange it for next weekend, if you like? Then you can meet my mate and his girlfriend."

"I'd like to," she began. "But next weekend I'm going home to see my parents. It's Dad's birthday."

"Oh," he managed.

"What about the weekend after?"

"It's a little far off. I'll talk to him and get back to you. Okay?"

"Yes."

Kevin had realised he had been too keen and his last comment had been to check himself. He would do his utmost to make the rowing happen.

"Ahhhh!" Sandra screamed, as a huge volume of water splashed over her. Kevin had hit the water rather flatly with the oar. It had certainly woken her from her dreamy state. He laughed and she scooped the river at him as fast as she could.

"Hey, hey, hey," he protested, around his laughter, trying to hit the water away from himself.

"I'm soaked," she said, pulling the cleaving blouse from her breasts.

"You'll dry out pretty soon."

"Thanks very much." But she was not too upset.

He began to row again, at first feigning another aggressive slap of water, but then assuming a slow stroke.

They were both quite wet.

"Tell me about your work," said Helen.

"What would you like to know? There's not much to tell."

"Oh, I don't know... Do you enjoy it?"

"Sometimes... It's a job, y'know."

She nodded, smiling.

"Better than being a miner," he said.

She nodded again.

"Some days work's real good. Y'know, you get stuck into a problem. Other days it's a real bore. Y'd get a pig's ear of a problem." Then he chuckled. "Whichever way you look at it, you get absolutely filthy. Not like your work, eh?"

"No. Definitely not."

He had heard all about her job. How it was a lot more than simply drawing the layout of a building. There were stresses, materials, lighting, foundations and all manner of things to consider. To Kevin her drawings looked like the cross-section drawings he sometimes found in the boxes of parts he opened. Not buildings at all.

She had told him how poorly paid she was. After seven years of study! He earned more than she did. But then, he had pointed out, if she had been earning more, she would not have been working in the pub and he would not have met her. She had blushed at this and a warm glow had filled him.

"How's your car going?" he asked. Her Dad had bought her a car.

"Much better now, thanks to your tune-up."

He smiled.

They were now on the path alongside the canal that, for a while, ran parallel to the river. It was so much more peaceful here. The main road seemed miles away.

An old woman approached and eventually passed them. Her lips had been thin like Beryl's and he began to think of Beryl.

She had been at the pub last night. But she had kept her place with her girlfriends over in the corner. He was with the boys. She knew what that meant. She also knew that if she hung around long enough, he would go to her.

Many times during the latter half of the evening he had caught her eye. And just a few minutes before the fight, through a gap in the crowd, he had actually smiled and winked at her. These occasional glimpses had been few and far between, due to the crowd and his making sure the boys did not catch on. Of course, they knew about her. But they did not know the full extent of their relationship. Even that was not completely true. Steve knew more than most.

"You know something, Kev? You're not only cock crazy, you're a bloody lucky bastard too. A regular Jack the lad."

In any case, he would have ended up in bed with her had it not been for the fight.

She'd probably gone on to the club hoping to find him there. Perhaps, if she had drunk enough she would have found someone to screw. But she always wanted him. Kevin knew he could oust any romance she could start up. He was top dog in her books. Yes, that was his position. Yet, he wanted her to meet someone. He felt sorry for her. She had such big, sad, cow-eyes. Such a pathetic person.

He had once said to her that she had sad eyes and she replied: "So have you."

"Have you always been good with your hands?" Helen asked, leading on from his enquiry about the condition of her car.

Kevin looked at her with a sly smile. For a second she

awaited his reply, then looked over and caught his naughty sideways grin. She laughed, a sort of puff and hit his side with the back of her hand.

She had hit his bruise and his smile vanished. He saw she was shocked by his reaction so he over-played it as if she had delivered a fatal blow. Seeing that he was play-acting she huffed and looked to the canal.

Kevin stumbled about a bit.

"I think you're going to have to give me the kiss of life."

"You should be so lucky," she said, again looking away from him to the canal.

He was not to be snubbed. The pain continued.

"Then we'll go together!" he exclaimed, grabbing her and pushing her towards the canal.

She shrieked: "Kevin!"

He held her fast, smiling, his mood in the balance.

"You're such a fool."

Her winning smile rescued him and he laughed.

There had been something intimate about her voicing his name. She was touching him, his being.

They walked on in silence.

The day seemed to be blossoming; the clouds dispersing, sounds becoming less acute whilst retaining their individuality.

Kevin still felt dull. A warm hand squeezed his forehead between his eyes.

Watching her from the corner of his eye, he rubbed his side.

The bastard's face was animal. Kevin was in a rage but he held himself. He knew what to do. Fast, real fast. Yank, crack and a knee to the groin. And as a final touch a full-bodied kick in the guts. Beautiful.

The table caught him at his side. His arm had toppled it. Drinks, beer mats, cigarette packets, ashtrays, the lot.

"I hardly touched you," Helen said, puzzled.

She had seen him.

"Yeah, I know. No. It wasn't you." His mind worked quickly. "We were lifting the head off a' E-type a couple of days ago. V12, you know. We needed a pulley." He looked at her and saw her concern. It was too much. He couldn't lay it on too thickly. "Well, it swung out when we had it in the air and hit me on the side."

"Really?" she said, but without disbelief.

"Yeah, look." He pulled up his T-shirt and showed her his bruise.

"Oooh," she exclaimed painfully.

Now he knew he had captured her.

"Why didn't you tell me"

"Huh? ... Well it's not the kind of thing you boast about."

"If something like that had happened to me, I would have told you."

Had he overdone it? Played it down too much?

"Ah, I'd have told you sooner or later. Just never had the opportunity."

A young couple overtook them. They were holding hands. She wore dungarees and a T-shirt, he jeans and a sleeveless T-shirt.

"I don't like his T-shirt," she said.

"It's all right," he remarked. He had quite a few like it.

He liked T-shirts to show off the body or he liked them to be baggy. For himself, he liked to show off his biceps. Her not liking that kind of thing said something about her. Another indication of their differences.

"You can always tell people by what they wear."

"Yeah?"

"Not necessarily what kind of jobs they do, but the kind of lifestyle they lead. Those two would be health food, CND supporters, driving - if they've got a car - a beat-up Renault 6 or better still a 2 CV."

He laughed.

"Yes," he agreed. He was glad she had taken the initiative because he felt too weak to be witty. Furthermore, he knew that the more he got her talking the more she would enjoy herself. He felt people loved talking; especially about themselves. They loved thinking themselves clever. So he'd prompt her to continue by enjoying her wit.

"Muesli-eaters," he added.

She smiled.

But the conversation dried up because there was no one else they could criticise. He saw her glance around and immediately felt the burden of silence upon himself. He had to think of something to say.

"Do you eat breakfast?" he asked.

"Yes," she replied, obviously pleased with the conversation, if not a little taken aback. "Just a bowl of cereal, a slice of toast and a cup of tea, usually."

"I time it just right," he said. "All I get is a cup of coffee. I'm not really a tea drinker." He paused. "Then about half-eight one of us goes over the tuck shop, over the road from the garage, and buys the cakes for our morning break."

She smiled. How he loved her smile!

"When I was a kid," he went on, "Mum used to force us to have breakfast. It was always tea and toast. Sometimes an egg."

"Really?"

"Yeah... Mum and Dad were real big tea drinkers.

Maybe that's why I don't drink it much now." Suddenly he became very self-conscious. He was doing all the talking.

"How about you?" he asked.

"What?"

"When you were a kid."

"Oh, sorry." Her hair was suffused by the light. As if an aura surrounded her head. It drenched her fair complexion in brilliance, exposing her freckles, her large eyes and the sharp angle of her nose.

For Kevin the sun was torture. It beat his aching head, magnifying the buzz.

"Like most memories," she began, "being a kid is full of nostalgia. You remember only the good times or the particularly bad times."

Was she about to say something awful? he wondered. Had he touched on a sensitive subject?

"The good times are a mixture of melancholy and happiness," she went on.

He nodded, totally at a loss as to where she was going or what mood had taken her.

"I spent quite a bit of time in a boarding school. So my memories of home are restricted to the school breaks."

Kevin didn't like her distant tone and he found himself cutting in.

"What was boarding school like?"

"Oh," she exclaimed. "It was all right. You get used to anything. We were pretty wild. But by today's standards it was all rather tame."

"Like what?"

"Like smoking in the toilets, skipping into town when we were supposed to be in bed. That sort of thing."

He smiled, although he was only half-listening. Ha! He could tell her of his comprehensive schooling. The teachers getting the girls pregnant, the smoking of dope on the common and the stabbings.

"My favourite subject was art," she was saying.

A sparrow swooped and rose before them. It seemed to break their individual reveries.

"What was your favourite subject?"

"I guess, Maths."

"Really?"

"No, I was lying," he joked.

"Oh, come on," she smiled.

"Well, you questioned it."

"It's a figure of speech."

"Really?"

"Yes." And then she realised what he had done and once again laughed and slapped his side. "Kevin, you fool!"

His bruise throbbed, but his humour ignored it.

She realised she may have hurt him and turned to him, the blood rushing to her face.

"I'm sorry, did I hurt you again?" Her fingertips, conveying her genuine concern, touched his forearm.

"It's okay," he replied.

For an instant their eyes met. Embarrassment took her and he was injured.

"But maybe we should swap sides," he suggested.

She made a move to do so, but with a gesture he stopped her.

"I was only joking. It's okay."

There was a short silence as they hastened to recover themselves.

"Was Maths really your favourite subject?" she asked.

"Not the alpha, beta, gamma stuff. I was pretty good with numbers." Yes, he had a flare for numbers in a practical way. None of the poncy alpha, beta, gamma stuff.

Most academics he'd come across just had no common-sense. Their heads were full of useless abstracts. Just look at one of them adding up a darts score. Not a clue.

"But you didn't stay on?"

"Naw, I wanted to get out and make money." He'd almost said yes and that he'd got a degree, knowing full well that she knew he had not. But he sensed he'd kidded around too much.

"Do you regret that now?"

"No, I don't think so. Sometimes, maybe. But I do all right. It's experience that counts in the real world. Besides, I'm quite happy where I am." Was he?

After a short time he continued.

"We had some fun at school. The teachers weren't up to much. The classes were too big, that sort of thing, you know. Me and my mates used to tease the professors - that's what we used to call the boffins, the clever kids... Oh, not in a horrible way," he lied, "just little pranks. Something to give the day a little life, you know, a little laugh." However, some of his mates had done more than tease. They'd given kids a dead-leg: a knee to the side of the thigh. Or, if in single file, they'd cup their hands behind them and pull up the crutch of the kid behind. He was right about the teachers. The English teacher was good but always tipsy; a failed lawyer. And the Geography teacher was a manic-depressive. She'd had a mental breakdown in the end. The work for most of them must have been soul-destroying. The classes were too big and the school was too big. And there were too many cut-backs. Short-changing the bleak future of the country.

He slapped the others face. Jeering voices rose. But Kevin did not hear what they were saying. He was afire with purpose. Yet, he was ashamed, because the boy before him would not fight and this was the third time Kevin had smacked him across the chops. Spurred on by the crowd. Now the boy's lip was cut. Kevin didn't want to fight. He hoped the boy would not blow because he didn't want to hurt him.

He would never forget that incident in the cloakroom. He had forgotten how he'd got into the situation and what the fight was about. Only the shame remained.

Caged

Locked.
Caged.
Staring.
Pacing.

Mocked.
Enraged.
Glaring.
Racing.

Locked.
Staged.
Swearing.
Wasting.

"Sounds a rough school," she remarked.

They were both distracted by the pub and the patrons around it. Some sat on the grassy bank beside the canal, others sat on the other side of the path against the wall or the fence of a neighbouring building.

The pub itself was an outsized, two storey cottage in appearance. By nature it had been an inn of sorts, with a paved courtyard out back for carriages, and no doubt at one time stables for horses. Ground level was below the canal and path, where the gardens and courtyard, now occupied by cumbersome, thick wood tables, surrounded the pub. The first floor entrance opened onto the pathway, but the bar was on the ground floor.

"Hungry?" he asked.

"Starving."

"Good."

A sudden fear stole Kevin. What if someone he knew were here! Worse still, what if the stranger was here!

"You look at my woman again I'll put you in an oxygen tent!" he had threatened.

"Yeah, you and whose fuckin' army?"

"Don't you?" asked Helen.

"Sorry, what? I was miles away."

"I like this pub."

"Yes. It's one of my favourites."

"Far enough to be out of town and close enough to walk to."

"Yes."

Helen and Kevin fell silent as they made their way along the path to the steps down to the small paved area in front of the pub.

Kevin was very conscious of everyone. He made cursory sweeps of the groups. Some were couples, others were groups of people and some were families, their kids running about beneath the small hump-backed bridge of large, irregular, stone blocks that skirted the canal.

By comparison the inside of the pub was dull and it took them a few seconds to adjust to the lack of light.

There was a great press of people up at the bar. In places it was three-deep.

"Blimey, it's packed!" he remarked to Helen as he dug into his front pocket. He produced a tight wad of notes and disentangled a fiver. He didn't carry a wallet. Armed with this crumpled note he turned to the bar and held it up as if it were a betting slip at the races.

"What'd you like?" he asked, holding his position in the passive aggression of the crowd.

"Half a cider, please," she returned. And her attention wandered once again to view the crowd about her, both standing and those at the shiny, dark-wood circular tables by the thick-glass, leaded windows.

"I can't see the menu," he said.

"A cottage cheese ploughman's will do, thanks."

He nodded as he turned to muscle-in closer.

Kevin could see he wouldn't be served for a while and looked at Helen. Yes, he thought, she was good-looking. She could dress a little better. But then, he liked girls to dress sexily, perhaps a little tarty. That certainly wouldn't be her. And what about make-up? She didn't wear much. That was good. You'd know what you'd be waking up with. But if she did something subtle with her eyes. Well, wow!

A glint of metal caught his eye and he looked over to the two old men by the window examining a candlestick holder.

"How old are you?" the middle-aged woman had asked, as she made her way to leave.

"Old enough," he had replied with a smile of contempt.

"He shouldn't be here," said the woman to his mates.

"Ah, go on with you, old woman," said John.

A ripple of uneasy laughter took the group.

"There was a candle in that holder." She pointed to

the alcove nearest Kevin.

"Was there?" said Martin.

"Yes. And he's taken it," she accused, pointing directly at Kevin, who, in his drunkenness, could only smile stupidly.

A silence followed. The woman stood there awkwardly and the group ignored her, quietly supping their pints.

Eventually she huffed, shook her head in disgust, loathing Kevin and then the others for seemingly leading him astray, and then she left.

Drink had detached Kevin, but he had still been amused. The funny thing was, was that he was not under age. To think that when he had been under age he had never been challenged. Yes, his mates had been older, a long-gone group from the early garage days. Where were they all now? Martin, John, Greasy?

He had taken the candle. What for? For no reason other than drink did that to him. Kleptomania.

"Next?"

"Pint of best and half a cider," he said, between the two chaps.

"Dry or sweet?" asked the girl, as she picked a sleever from the overhead shelves.

"Dry," he guessed. It was too difficult to turn and ask Helen who had been forced away from him by the others trying to get to the bar.

He then ordered the food, choosing a steak and kidney pie and chips for himself. He gave the girl his surname and paid for the lot.

After receiving the change and a receipt for the food he backed away from the bar with the drinks in his hand.

"Thanks," Helen said, when she took her drink from

him. He'd already supped the top off his at the bar.

"Outside?" he asked.

"Yes, I think so," she replied.

The brightness made them squint. A whole range of people occupied the tables in the immediate area. From old age pensioners to young couples, to students, the trendy and the indifferent. It was a complete cross-section of the community, and the variety and colours of their dress also highlighted the fact that the entire spectrum of society was represented here.

Once again Kevin was acutely aware of the possibility of running into someone he knew.

"I think we'd be better off up by the canal," he said.

She nodded and made her way up to the steps. He followed watching all about him from the periphery of his vision. It seemed to him that newcomers were unwelcome. As if, until you found a place, you were an outsider. The crowd was hostile. He'd be happier when they found a place and were accepted by the pub. So arrogance sat behind his eyes and aggression tightened his shoulders.

At canal level they looked up and down the path.

"Pretty crowded," she remarked.

He nodded, scrutinising the faces at the same time as searching for a place.

"How about there?" he pointed.

"Fine."

He took a sip of his beer as she set off towards the area he had suggested. How nicely she moved in jeans, her buttocks tight and horse-like, arousing something basic in him.

Then he saw the redheaded woman with the fair-haired child. Could it be Rita? No, surely Rita was not so rounded? Unlike Beryl he knew she would not stay away.

She would be disruptive and try to make some kind of claim on him.

"Oh Kevin, Kevin, only you. Only you," she had gasped as he moved over her.

He had shied from her, inside himself. Her over-the-top affection - instant, desperately sincere, and yet unnatural in its spontaneity - had caused his being to shrink from her.

Her dope smoking, the love-bite she had marked him with and her child, all these things alienated him. They turned him cold inside. She was saying: "Walk over me." It was written all over her face. She had been shattered by her husband. He had left her. And now she craved to be hurt again. Strange. Her heart knew it was hopeless with him, but she had given herself up to hopelessness. Hopelessness was her companion.

And Kevin knew that to stay with her too long would make him hopeless also. He would have to break free. Yes, he'd finish it next week. Nip it in the bud.

The redheaded woman turned and Kevin saw her face. How could he have thought she could be Rita? Rita was older than him, but not that old. Rita was also terribly good-looking.

They sat on the grass by the fence, their feet stretched out before them just reaching the path. A couple sat to their left and three lads, possibly students, stood to their right.

"That's better," she said when they were seated comfortably. "I always forget how packed this pub gets until I'm here."

"Yeah," he nodded. "You get a good drop here, you see."

She smiled.

An easy silence followed in which they took sips

from their drinks. Kevin had already drunk a third of his pint. Although the thought of beer had repulsed him, he was awfully thirsty and drank it easily, as if it were Adam's ale.

She obviously noticed his rapid consumption.

"You do like your beer, don't you?"

"Just thirsty."

"I thought you were feeling under the weather."

"I am. Hair of the dog, you know."

She smiled again, the dimples appearing just beyond the limits of her lips.

A kid yelped and they looked over.

"Noisy, aren't they?" he remarked, stopping himself from saying: "Noisy bleeders, aren't they?"

"Yes. I don't know how their parents put up with them."

"Won't you have kids when you get married?"

"No, I don't think so."

"Why not?"

"I guess it's partly to do with my career. Also I have no desire to have them."

"Oh. But your husband'd have some say?"

"Yes. It's something we'd have to work out. Why? Would you have kids?"

He had hoped she would not ask. Yes, he wanted kids.

"Eventually I would. I'd like to live a little first, with my wife."

"Fair enough."

Kevin did not like the difference of opinion. It nettled him.

"That's assuming I get married," he went on.

"You don't think you will?"

"I don't know. I suppose somebody'll come along eventually. There's no hurry."

"Not for you," she began. "For women who want kids there is."

"How come a nice girl like you is not going out with someone?"

She blushed.

Of course he knew the answer. Nobody had got off their butts to ask her. She rarely went to discos and wasn't keen on the types that hung around them. Most of her fellow workers were married.

"I don't know."

He had embarrassed her with his compliment.

"It's no big deal," he backtracked.

"Maybe," she said distantly.

Oh, what had he done now? he wondered.

"I think it's good to be going out with someone," she said. "The older you get the more set in your ways you become. You get more fussy and intolerant."

"You really think so?" Could he go out with her? She was so nice. Too nice? And yet, her serious side frightened him. It was so grave.

"Yes."

"Hmmmm."

Another pause ensued and they drank.

"Have you been out with many women?"

"Yes." Shit, more distance.

"How many?"

"I don't know."

"About?"

"I really couldn't say. Loads."

"Oh."

He looked to her. She was drawing away from him.

How clumsy he was.

"It depends what you mean by going out with?"

"Proper girlfriends."

"Well, only about six have lasted more than three months."

She nodded.

"And you?"

"I've only had four boyfriends to speak of."

Pause.

So, what had all that been about? Another dead-end subject. Had she merely been making conversation?

"One of them wanted to marry me."

"Don't sound so surprised," he chuckled.

She smiled.

"Why didn't you?"

"It wasn't right."

"Aha. If it had been, would you have got married in a church?"

"Yes, I think so."

"Yeah, I'd like to get married in a church. It's romantic."

"It's more than romantic," she said.

"What do you mean?"

"Well, it's God's blessing, of course."

A cloud crossed his face and he fell silent.

"Don't you believe in God?" she pursued.

"No," he said in a small voice.

"Don't sound so ashamed. Everyone's entitled to their opinion. I believe, but I don't frequent a church or practice in any way."

"I guess it's good to believe in something. But I just can't rationalise something so, er..."

"Why rationalise?" she asked, as he searched for his

word. "Why not feel it? Believe it?"

"I can't."

"That's fair enough."

"Is it? It'd be so nice to put it all down to God. Then you've got no responsibility."

"Oh, I wouldn't say that. You've got a great responsibility to God."

"Yes, but whatever happens to you, you can put it down to God's will."

"That's not true. That's fate. A totally different matter. There's a subtle difference. The word of God, the Bible, is a guide. The will of God is written there. You decide whether to follow or not."

"Cor blimey, this is heavy," he smiled, not sure that he understood the difference. She smiled too.

"It's good to talk like this sometimes," she said.

"Yes, I suppose so. But with religion, things can become quite heated."

"I don't think that'll happen here."

"No."

He looked at her drink and decided to slow down a little. The dullness rose up in him.

"You know where cor blimey comes from, don't you?" she asked.

He looked at her.

"It's from: God blind me," she said. "Still an exclamation."

A welcome breeze moved across them. The sun had been unimpeded by cloud for some time.

Kevin decided to exert his will. He wanted to impress her with his opinions. Yet, he was hesitant, for the subject could alienate him further from her.

"If there is a God, do you think He'd let all these

miserable things go on?"

"The misery is brought on by Man."

He felt as if he were to blame in some way.

"Yes, but some of the problems are beyond Man's control."

"Such as?"

He was about to mention the starving millions, war, poverty and the like, but each time he realised that Man was to blame. Kevin felt defeated, even a little humiliated.

"Maybe you're right," he admitted. Oh, why were his thinking capabilities so crappy today? The hangover, of course. Even so, he should be able to do better than this. He was beginning to look like an ignorant fool and that was the worse thing that could happen.

"I suppose," he ventured, "I do believe there must be something greater. It just seems a little simple to call it God?"

"Simple!"

Shit! He laughed nervously. "Well, Man's interpretation. All this miracle stuff. Ah, I don't know." Did he really have any fixed opinions?

She must have realised that he was floundering and not enjoying the conversation, for she closed it off.

"You believe in something greater, so we'll leave it at that."

A mercy killing.

After they'd taken the lull in the conversation to drink, Kevin, strangely, brought up the subject again. Sod it, he would not be crushed.

"I must admit I like U2 and they're a -" he was about to say God-squad "- Christian band."

"Yes, they are very good."

"What kind of music do you like?"

The three lads suddenly burst into laughter and Kevin's focus of attention was shifted momentarily. What was the joke?

"That's brilliant," one of them said. Then Kevin could not catch what they were saying.

"All sorts," Helen replied.

"Like?" he persisted, returning all his attention to her.

"Roxy, Bowie, Sade."

She likes polished, smoother music, he thought.

"I also like classical," she went on.

Pause.

He knew she was waiting for some kind of response.

"I've got The Planets, but that's all. I like the popular stuff, though. You know, Beethoven."

"Beethoven's fifth."

"Yes, that sort of thing," he replied unsure, but it sounded right.

"I'll lend you some of my records," she offered.

"Yes, that'll be nice." He hoped that they would not be too heavy, like the books of Satre and Hamsun, indigestible.

The dullness flared up in him and he drifted from them, all the while he tried to fake his attentiveness. He drifted to nowhere. To the beetle scampering along the path, to the tiny snake-like mound of dirt - from a worm hole - to the man with the big thighs making paper boats for the child, to the rustling trees, so still and then swishing when the breeze rose, to the chirping of the birds, back to check the progress of the beetle and up to the vapour trail of the silent plane overhead.

Out of all this he heard his surname being called.

"Yes," he answered, raising his hand to the girl carrying their food.

He stood, showed the receipt and took the plates, serviettes and cutlery from her.

"There we are," he said, handing Helen hers and seating himself.

For a moment they ate in silence, she with the plate on her lap, he with it at his side, on the ground.

He knew the food would sustain him and, hopefully, revive him.

Kevin still felt he was isolated in an electric pain. It was a curtain of buzzing that shrouded his perception, despite his observation of all about him.

Once again he was ill at ease. He felt that he should assert himself.

"Unlike most people," he began, round a chip, "I don't like The Beatles."

"No?" There was no surprise in her voice.

"No. I find them depressing. Although, when I was a kid I liked them. Collected the bubble-gum cards and all."

She smiled and he was spurred on.

"You'll laugh," he continued, with a broad grin on his face. "But me and my brothers and sisters used to imitate The Beatles. Trouble is, all four of us - there were four of us then -"

"You've got two sisters and two brothers?"

"Yes, five of us altogether."

"Quite evenly balanced."

"Yeah, I guess so."

There was a moment's pause. He was determined to continue with his story.

"Anyway, the four of us -"

"Yes."

"- had these plastic tennis racquets, even the strings were thick plastic. One solid, moulded mass of green or yellow. They were our guitars, see. And we used to sing: She loves you, yeah, yeah, yeah. I think that's all the words we knew."

She chuckled.

"No one wanted to be the drummer. So we had four guitarists. Our parents used to get us to play in front of our relatives."

Helen then told a story of when her sister and herself had dressed up and enacted a pantomime for their aunt.

"Would you like to try some of this pie?" he asked, after a pause.

"No thanks... Would you like to try some of this salad?"

"No. I'm not a rabbit... I'll get you another drink in a minute."

"I'll buy them."

"No. It's okay."

"But you bought the last round and this food. You must let me pay."

"Nope."

"I insist."

"Nope."

"Well then, I don't want one."

"What?"

"I don't want another drink."

"I'll tell you what, I'll buy the next and you can buy the one after."

"How long are we going to be here? There's not enough time, is there?"

"Yes."

"You're lying -"

"No, I'm sitting."

"Kevin. Don't muck around. I don't think there's

enough time. I'll buy the next round. I really insist."

"Okay, okay."

"But you have to go and get them."

And he laughed. And she smiled.

A fly hovered about his food. He brushed at it. It circled and returned, looking for a suitable landing place. He brushed at it again, more violently this time, hoping to strike it. It flew a slightly greater distance, returned for another brush-off and disappeared from sight.

Soon he had finished his food and she reached into her bag and produced a fiver.

"Here."

"Thanks," he replied, taking the money and feeling a twinge of embarrassment.

"Don't get embarrassed," she smiled, setting her bag down.

He snorted. Boy, she was so sensitive to register something he thought did not show.

At that moment he liked her a lot. She was not stupid. And she had bottle. She said what she wanted. Not shy at all. Quite willing to voice her opinion.

He would have been quite content to sit there for a long time to come, but he knew that he must get the drinks. Otherwise she'd question him and that would spoil his contentment. However, to get up he had to break free of the feeling.

"Right," he said boisterously, and he abruptly rose.

He took up his glass and she passed her own, looking up at him, squinting, for the sun was behind him. Her features were awash with sunlight. Her face flattened, her hair radiant, blessed again, and for a second he could smell the very freshness her appearance evoked.

She was smiling, although she could not see his face.

Ah, sunshine was made for her.

The buzzing was distant and his being was light. He could bound the canal in a single leap. Yes, easily. The wind would carry him. But he needn't impress her with such boyish acts. In any case, no mortal man could actually jump the canal. He'd get less than half way. That would really impress her! Oh, but to make her laugh was to make his heart leap.

"Same again?"

"Please." Then, "thank you, Kevin."

Kevin. Kevin. His name again! Voiced by her! It touched him.

He left, oblivious of the patrons, the sunlight sparkling on the canal with painful intensity and the subtle motion of nature: twitch of grass, shiver of leaf, flutter of wing, swing of fly; the knowing smile of living harmony.

He felt marvellously alive. The sun brought out such colours in people. Most of the time the passionate moodiness of Britain's climate made the people downtrodden, blue-grey and hunched. It beat down on them; weathered them. They reflected the weather in their faces and attitudes; a slate dullness lay in their eyes. But days like these emancipated them, lifted and released them. A relaxation took them and they indulged themselves, continental-like. The sun shone in their faces and sparkled in their eyes.

In this frame of mind he bought the drinks.

On his way back, before reaching the steps up to the path, somebody called his name. He turned, a drink in each hand, recognised a friend sitting with two strangers, gave a smile, a quick: "all right, Paul?" lifted his drinks and continued on his way.

He prayed that that'd be sufficiently polite and

enough to convey his wish to be left out. It was dangerous, he knew, precarious and unsettling as gangs of kids can sometimes be. He didn't really want to be disturbed. Was Paul astute enough to realise this? Kevin was not sure.

As he walked up to her he felt awkward and clumsy. Especially carrying the drinks in separate hands. Like some nancy-boy. With the lads he'd carry two pint-mugs in each fist or three sleevers between two palms. He could not do that here. The glasses were different sizes.

He wanted to look down himself, at his feet. He wanted to check his gut. Perhaps pull it in, subtly, slightly. He was not sure. What did she see? Ah, sod it. He wouldn't go soft. He had a good body. He kept himself in trim. Don't swagger. It was like walking along some damned catwalk. Were those three students eyeing him? Yes, he was with her. Tough shit. Probably benders, anyway.

"Are you okay?" she asked, when he'd sat down beside her.

"Yeah," he smiled. Shit. "Why?"

"You looked angry about something."

"Angry? Naw... Oh, here's your change before I forget." He went to his pocket, irritated by his self-consciousness.

"Oh. I'd forgotten."

"Right. Let's forget it then," he suggested, reaching for his pint.

She slapped his thigh, a broad grin on her face.

He laughed, a little uneasily, and dug into his pocket again.

"Please let me give you something for the food."

"Don't start that again."

"Okay. Thanks very much, Kevin."

After giving her her change a silence took them.

Kevin felt that Helen was taking in the day as he was doing. Therefore the silence was not empty. Then it began to nag on him. And he thought of the married couples he'd seen in pubs sitting with absolutely nothing to say to each other.

"Real friends are not embarrassed by silence," he said.

She nodded.

"I mean," he went on, "some people find it real awkward."

She smiled.

And he continued, trying to keep his smile away. "It's just so nice to sit here in silence and watch the day. Some people miss it all. They just ruin it by talking. Going on and on and on -"

She let out a gasp of a laugh as if she'd been holding her breath. A kind of exasperated, humorous sigh.

"Okay, okay," she said.

Levity hung in the silence that followed.

My reflection

I look more like myself
Than my reflection does.

My reflection is alien to me,
It gives me no more.
My reflection is in cold glass.
It absorbs my love,
Repels my hate,
Absorbs my happiness,
Reflects my sorrow.

It says to me,

As if to say to you:
"I will give no more
Than you give me.
I will love no more
Than you love me."

My reflection is only part of me.

"Did you ever see Local Hero?" she asked.

"Yes. It was really funny."

"A bit hard on the Americans."

"Yeah, I suppose. Perhaps they deserve it? Anyway, it was funny in an easy sort of way."

"I know what you mean. Not madcap and zany like such a lot of films."

He nodded.

"Have you seen the Rockys?" he ventured.

"I've seen Rocky one."

"What? When it came on the box?"

"Yes."

"What did you think?"

"I was pleasantly surprised."

A positive response.

"The other two are just as good. Ah, they're pretty basic. You know, all the right ingredients, but I think they're good... Good clean fun."

"Entertainment."

"Yeah. Nothing more, nothing less."

Had something subtle transpired here? Was she humouring him? Did she like her films like she liked her books?

Without losing momentum he sent out a probe.

"Ever seen the film Francés?"

"Yes. It was harrowing, wasn't it?"

"Especially as it was true."

Then they went on to discuss the film in more detail. They talked about other sequences in other films. And they talked of favourite films, actors and actresses.

"Too bad life isn't like films," he suddenly said.

"I don't know. Some films are not too appealing. I'm glad they're just films."

"Yeah." He looked pensively into his pint. The levity had dissipated.

"What I mean is," he began, shakily, "is that we all go our different ways. It's sort of unpredictable. It's not a film. There needn't be a meaning or a happy ending. Or a proper ending."

She nodded.

However, Kevin felt he was not reaching her. Only if he were more eloquent. Only if...

"I read somewhere," she said, "that children are like colours. They have all the colours."

"What do you mean?"

"We all start off with a complete range of colours. Like a rainbow. Age and experience blemish them. They're all in bands and they begin to merge and the boundaries become less definite -"

"So the colours are like your character."

"Yes, that's it. Your emotions, your personality. Things that drive you. And as you grow certain colours or one colour, become dominant."

"I guess that makes me brown, then," he laughed.

"Oh no," she exclaimed. "You're more red or orange."

"Reddish brown?"

"No, you've got orange. Happy and easy."

"And you? How do you see yourself?"

"Blue."

"No. I don't think you're one colour."

"I do. A sort of deep blue."

"Nope. You have green and light blue and a touch of pink and yellow. Feminine."

"Let's beg to differ on that."

"Okay."

Pause.

"Look there!" he said, pointing across the canal. "A squirrel. See it?"

"Yes."

In little bounds the grey creature hopped up a tree.

"I bet he ain't worried about what colour he is," he remarked, lightly.

"No," she smiled. "People are such complicated creatures. Sometimes I wish I were an animal."

"Like what?"

"Like, er, a ... a squirrel would do."

"What? Collecting nuts all day? Most women do that already."

"Ooooh, Kevin." She thumped him as he laughed at his pun.

Perhaps the drink was taking effect? He would never have said anything as bold earlier. What did it matter? She was smiling. You've got to have a laugh.

His jovial manner was not to be put down, despite her apparent shock. Or possibly he was trying to cover his rudeness? Was he trying to race on and bury it?

"I'd have thought you'd have come back as a rabbit."

"Why?"

He realised that he could be lining her up for a rude comment. "'cause you've got lovely eyes and you're cute and cuddly." Dumb. Dumb.

She smiled and to hide her embarrassment she asked him what he would like to come back as, humans aside.

"Oh, I don't know. A wolf or something I s'pose."

"That's a bit aggressive. If it has to be a dog, why don't you settle for a poodle?"

"Cor blimey," he laughed. "Now I should hit you."

A breeze caused the branches of the trees to sway, the leaves waving frantically. Feather light white clouds, soft as breath, moved across the pastel blue sky. They seemed to expand and spread as they went overhead. Yet, their shape remained.

A small bird raced over the treetops, ceased beating its wings, dipped suddenly as if to move under some invisible object, then, rapidly beating its wings once again, shot up to its original elevation.

Upon the wall of a small sandstone cottage opposite, in the shadow of a large tree through which the sun shone, light, like individual flames, danced and shifted and disappeared and blinked. It was a continuous, natural, light show. Like the sprinkling of rain, the rage of a fire, the ripples on a pond and the blankness of a wall.

Kevin was totally aware. It was almost intense. The hangover was gone. During this peaceful moment he heard no songs, indulged no memories, fought no battles and wandered nowhere. He was appreciating the scheme of things. He was with Helen. It was happening now.

The moment was wondrous, simply because it was insignificant. It was a collection of insignificances. Given significance through his observation. A feeling. A momentous whisper from Nature to him. An incomprehensible clue to the enigma of life. Soon to be a memory. All too soon. He could feel it becoming a memory as he indulged it and he relished the living moment all the more, almost as if he could stave off its slow fossilisation in his mind. Or, as if he could indulge every little facet of its make-up, so that the fossilisation would be more accurate. Perfect and more alive than most memories. Then he could enjoy the feeling it evoked at his leisure without melancholy or nostalgia. But he began to grapple in his effort to capture it all. It was slipping away from him. And the more he struggled, like a fish in a net, the more entangled he became, the more tighter he was held as time took the moment away from him.

Then it was gone.

Kevin looked at the young family as they passed by. Mother, father and little girl. A blond, naïve little thing. A rainbow child full of sunshine. The parents were easy and relaxed. At that moment he yearned for their lifestyle. He felt that he would be more complete. But the moment passed when he thought of the possible hassle. Was it such a high price to pay? Did one truly pay a price? Could Helen truly not want children?

The young family strolled on. The child fluttering about the unfaltering parents like Nature's new-born innocence.

"Nice family," she remarked.

"Yes," he agreed, but ventured no further.

When the young couple to their left made ready to leave, he noticed that the three lads had gone.

Last orders were never called outside the pub, so he had had no feel for the time. A glance at his watch told him of its incredible passing.

She must have noticed for she made the following enquiry: "Have you got much to do this afternoon?"

"I was going to go into town, but now I don't think

I'll bother. I'll go Monday lunchtime."

Pause.

"I was going to do a little work. There's no hurry, though," she stated.

"I may go weight-training. Feeling a little podgy."

"You're joking?" she laughed.

"No. Look at this." He pinched a quantity of his waist.

"Anyone can do that."

"Well, I don't like it."

"Okay. It's good to keep in trim."

"Yeah. It's how you feel that's important."

He sipped his drink, then asked: "Do you do any exercise?"

"I go to aerobics when I can. And sometimes a swim. Nothing regular though. I'm working up to three times a week.

"I do something almost everyday. If I miss weight training after work, you know, if it was a hard graft at work, then I go for a run. I sometimes go swimming, but it's such an effort to go. A real palaver. Perhaps we can go together sometime?"

"Yes." Then, "I used to do judo."

"Bloody 'ell, I won't tangle with you."

"I didn't get very far. I only did it for two years and that was on and off. I've forgotten it all now."

"I bet you know some useful leg-locks," he laughed.

"Kevin," she exclaimed. "I don't know, you are so cheeky today." She blushed deeply.

He fell silent, crushed. His gallows humour was too vicious for her. But Kevin still felt women liked a certain arrogance. A strong personality. Not annihilating. As people turned to the sun, so he thought people should be brilliant and bright to be attractive. Of course he could not always be so. But even in this moment of deflation he knew he would have to quickly flare-up. He could not afford to be extinguished.

"I just feel good. Must be something to do with the company."

She blushed still deeper.

"Come on, you're getting drunk."

"After one and a half pints? You've gotta be joking."

"I think you're topping up from last night."

He laughed and she smiled.

"No, seriously," he began. "I do feel relaxed with you. It's easy." Yet, very deep down he felt uneasy. He'd only tasted trust once and that had been with Sandra, over two years ago. But here, something elemental was not right. Was he lying to himself? Did he want to love her rather than feel he loved her?

"I like you too," she said.

Of course she did. He was exciting and unpredictable. Ah, but to get her in the sack. Then he'd show her how exciting things could be. Then again, would it spoil this innocence and easy banter? He liked it like this. To bed her would be to conquer her. Did he want that? Yes and no. Ha! What did she feel about him? Could he really charm her to bed? He hadn't even got her into his flat let alone his sports room.

He resolved to give her a good kiss when he left her today. He'd know then.

Kevin looked at her drink. She'd almost finished. Another two gulps and he'd be finished too.

"This is nice," he remarked.

"Yes."

"Just sitting here in the sunshine. Do you fancy a

walk? I think there're some benches further up the path. I mean, you don't want to go back yet, do you?"

"No. A walk would be lovely. Not too far, though. It's getting pretty hot. The wind's dropping."

He gulped his beer. One. Two.

"Okay?" he asked, when she'd finished her drink.

"Yes, thanks."

They both got up and brushed bits of grass from themselves.

Strangely enough, he did feel rather light-headed. It was a good feeling.

A few groups of people were dotted around. They were visited by a come-on-drink-up-please-let's-have-those-glasses landlord carrying a tray of empties. Relatively, the area was barren. This added a strange devastation to the place. Like that at the end of a party.

Slowly they made their way along the canal-side, passed the pub, under the bridge.

Paul had gone and Kevin's momentary anxiety disappeared, making him all the more light.

The sound of the Eurythmics *Sweet Dreams* came from the pub. He didn't hear the lyrics, he only heard the jaunty tune, and so he was at a loss as to why the following memory occurred.

"I've managed to get off my shift. Do you fancy going out for a drink?"

"Actually," he began, "there's a program on telly I'd like to see."

"So you don't want to see me?"

"Well, I saw you yesterday."

"It's not that often I get off a shift. What's the matter with me? Have I grown two heads?"

"No, don't be silly." He couldn't imagine Beryl with

two heads. "I just fancy staying in tonight."

"Didn't you enjoy it last night?"

"'course I did. Be reasonable, will you?"

"Me, be reasonable!"

Silence.

"Is that it, then?" she asked, viciously quiet.

"I just want to stay in tonight," he returned, putting a slight plea in his voice.

"Fine." And the phone was slammed down.

That had been about a week after he had met her at the disco. She'd asked him to dance. She had rapidly got heavy and more demanding, and he'd run. The phone conversation had been the first acknowledgement of their differing attitudes.

Three days later a note from her arrived. He'd replied and then she'd telephoned. They'd gone out for a drink and agreed to part as friends. But when it came to dropping her at her place, having walked her home, she'd asked for a kiss.

"No, a proper one."

"Okay."

"Come in for coffee."

"No, I must get back."

"I won't keep you long."

He faltered and she opened her front door.

"Come on."

Drink had made him weak and he had stayed the night. In the morning he had hated himself. After all they'd said in the pub.

"The world's full of lads and lassies. And I mean the four-legged kind," remarked Tony.

Leaving her he had said he would call her sometime and he had watched her eyes glaze over.

So it went on. On and off. She became more and

more pathetic. Throwing herself at him periodically. Then he realised he was just as weak. Each time he hated himself a little more, but at each opportunity to break free he was taken by drink and his thirst for flesh. For by now, they were quite used to each other in bed, and their sex was good.

It was still going on. About once a month. Always when he felt like it. When he hated himself. When he was drunk. When he hated the world. A few times he'd got blitzed with the boys and afterwards gone to her place, without considering whether she was with anyone, hammering on her door like some slobbering madman. And she took him in every time.

Currently, Rita was more of a headache to him. He had no control over their situation.

They had emerged from under the bridge into the sunlight.

"I hope my arms don't get burnt," Helen said.

"Naw, they're not even red."

"You're not likely to get burnt."

"No. Ever since a holiday in Greece over two years ago I've always kept a slight tan."

"That's the trouble with us of the fairer skin. As soon as we acquire a tan we lose it."

"Where have you been abroad?"

"Corfu, Crete, France, Spain, ... er, ... Yugoslavia and er, I think that's it. Most of my holidays have been here. Scotland, the lake district, Cornwall, Dorset."

He nodded.

"I haven't really done anywhere in England. Visiting friends for a weekend -" He thought of the Manchester weekend visiting an old school-mate and could not suppress a smile. He remembered the drunken night in the centre.

What a mess! One of the gang had turned the high street into a runway by setting all the plastic bins of the lampposts on fire. Kevin could see him now, running in the darkness down the middle of the road, his arms stretched out, pretending to be an aeroplane. "Used to visit granddad once a year till I was about fourteen. That was with the family, of course."

"Where?"

"Oh, yeah. Liverpool."

After a pause he went on.

"I've been to quite a few islands in Greece and I've been to the mainland. Er, last year I went to Australia. I was thinking of emigrating."

"Were you?"

"No, I was lying," he laughed.

She chuckled.

"Yes, I was."

"Are you going to?"

"Er, eventually I may. But not yet."

As they walked on they discussed his reasons for possibly emigrating, which inevitably led to the state of the country: Thatcher, the miners, Scargill. The country was going to pot. Young people were disillusioned. It was a rat race. People were scrambling over one another to get from the bottom. There again, they were more politically aware than their forefathers. The media gave the people what they wanted, they wanted to hear of their future, and this meant the government. This, in turn, exposed the government as a body of fallible people and not the noble leaders of old set apart from the mass. And this exposure compounded the mass disillusion.

Kevin surprised himself with his political opinions. However, he could propose no solution. As far as he was concerned it was a sign of the times. He had resigned himself to the fact that no matter who was in power they would not be able to stop the country from going to pot.

"There doesn't look like there's anywhere to sit," said Helen, coming to a halt.

It was true. The shrubbery that encroached the fence beside the path was hostile and unbroken.

"I think you're right," he agreed, looking down the path for a break in the bushes. "I felt sure there were some benches."

"Shall we turn back?"

"Yeah, sure," he replied, disappointed and slightly vexed.

The two of them were quite alone on the path. Way off in the distance a man was walking his dog. The sun brightened the countryside and darkened the shadows. They felt warmed to their very bones. So that when a cloud obscured the sun's rays and an icy hand touched their skin they remained warm inside.

Kevin wanted to prolong the day and extend his time with her. He felt desperate now that they were heading home.

"You must come to my place sometime. I'll cook you a meal."

"That'll be lovely, but not this week. I've got rather a lot to do before I go home."

"Yeah, sure, fine." There was a slight lack of enthusiasm in her voice and this was a blow to him.

"It's your own place, isn't it?"

"Yes. It's certainly better than renting. Really, it costs the same."

"I can't afford it just yet."

"Oh, I wouldn't have been able to afford it if my

father hadn't died."

The sea

Ever-changing shoreline,
You are the key to life.
You, the sea, grow from ripple,
To high and mighty wave.
Some ride the crest,
So big, so white
But some sink,
Some drown.
Then your life fades,
But you reach out to the very end.

"Hmmm, I'm sorry."

"Ahh, it's a couple o' years now... It's funny, but no one knows what to say when you mention death." Kevin allowed himself to take her into his confidence. For a few moments the easy, witty Kevin disappeared. "When an ex-girlfriend of mine was killed in a car crash, no one knew what to say." He was speaking of a girl he had met after his relationship with Sandra, in the wake of which he had not taken seriously. Only after she had left him did he realise what he had thrown away. She had earned his respect and he'd just begun to show an interest in her when she was killed. "It certainly hammered home the frailty of life... Huh, it really makes me angry when you see people wasting their lives, screwing themselves up over nothing... Relationships. That's a good one. Even the word is heavy and serious. Relationship. It's so permanent and binding. Why don't they call it fun or something? Something simple and light."

"You sound as though you don't approve."

"I don't like all the -" he was about to say shit "- crap that comes with them. People get so neurotic. He said this and she did that..."

"Oh Kevin, Kevin, only you. Only you," she had gasped as he moved over her. Push. Push. Push.

Then, as he had arched back to move deeper and break the rhythm, by a trick of the light through the curtains into the dark room, Rita's eyes had disappeared, her lovely high cheekbones had hollowed the sides of her face and for an instant he saw a skull. She had smiled and the show of teeth had been hideous. A death's head. Skin and bone. Animal.

Kevin had closed his eyes and pulled up the backs of her knees so that they rested on his biceps. Then he'd pushed, hoping to give her pain, hearing her gasp, sensing the wave of her feet. Push. Push. Push.

"Perhaps it's just the girls you've met," Helen put forth.

He nodded by way of reply.

Sandra and he were lying in bed. She was asleep in the foetal position, head upon his shoulder, bent knee near his crotch. He was awake, staring contentedly at the blackness above him, feeling the kiss of her breath on his chest. His arm was about her, his palm near the side of her breast.

Kevin moved his fingers slightly. His arm was aching, but he did not move. He knew her skin: its feel, its smell, its appearance, its taste. Her knew her. And he trusted her.

"And when two people get together," Helen went on, "one is bound to get more involved than the other."

"I guess so," Kevin agreed distantly.

"When two people meet they have to pass through the sexual barrier."

The phrase "sexual barrier" brought him back to her. "What do you mean?"

"Like us," she said. "We'll just be friends. When you meet someone of the opposite sex you have to pass through the crucial stage of whether or not you'll have physical relations with them."

He was reeling from the blow. Surely they had passed through no such barrier? Was this how she felt about him?

Stricken, Kevin's eyes became glass, shiny and hard.

Damn it! They'd passed through nothing! Ha, why couldn't she say sex instead of bleedin' physical relations? Maybe she was a stuck-up bitch after all! No, no. He was being too harsh. He didn't mean that. But they'd passed through no barrier. He'd win her over. The same way he won all his women over. Treat them with arrogance. Demand their respect. Occasionally do something soft and romantic. That really did them in.

He let her lead up the stairs. She was unsure on her feet and used the wall and banister to steady herself.

"Look son," his father had said, "if you're going to dip your wick, or whatever you call it nowadays, take precautions, eh?"

What to do? What to say?

"Sandra, I, er, wanted to be there," he said. Yes, he wanted to be punished too.

"I know," she replied. "I didn't expect them to take me in straight away. I only went to make an appointment."

"Are you okay?" he asked again.

"Yes. Still a little drugged up."

At the top of the stairs she opened her flat door.

Immediately she saw the bouquets of flowers and boxes of her favourite chocolates.

"Oh Kevin, I don't know what to say."

He had been genuinely surprised that she had been surprised. It had been all he could do when her flatmate had told him what she had had done. How he'd wanted to be there to share the burden of guilt. He'd make it up to her.

An awkward silence passed between Helen and Kevin.

The little hump-backed bridge of large, irregular, stone blocks was before them. From it three boys threw stones into the canal.

As they came out from under the bridge Kevin heard their quiet, racy voices. A few seconds later he saw them. They sat alone at a table near the steps, obviously arguing intensely. Other than this couple the pub area was deserted.

Kevin smiled and inside he laughed. The smile was for himself and he hid it from Helen.

Islands

People move with the seasons
Physical cycles
Sway the reasons

Life forces all around
In the air
Over the ground

Others shape your feeling
What to say
How much you're revealing

Islands are never mainlands
Never grow
Never gain lands.

He put himself in check by wondering whether he was being too cynical about relationships. Bloody hell, no way was he one of the walking wounded. Of course some relationships worked. Just look at Jane and Terry. Yeah, they argued; but they were together.

Kevin grew vague and distant. He no longer felt the touch of the day. This, in turn, made him wonder at his earlier feeling. What element had brought on the feeling? The tranquil sky? The violent play of light on the building? The trees? The water? The birds? Helen? He could not pinpoint the source of his feeling, but the remnants of it were still strong in him and they rose up and lifted him. He bounded back, uncaring and bold, and this pleased him.

"It's on days like these that it's great to be alive," he said, before noticing the gathering clouds on the horizon.

"Every day should be a celebration."

He laughed.

"What's so funny?" she asked.

"It just seemed like a naff thing to say."

"Well, I'm sorry," she said irritably.

"Ah, come on. Of course every day is great. But some are better than others. You must admit that?"

"Yes."

"Hey," he began, full of beans. "What do you call a contented cannibal?"

"I don't know," she returned, after the obligatory short pause.

"Someone who's fed up with people."

"Oh Kevin," she smiled, "that's horrible."

He laughed.

"It's the only clean one I know."

She smiled again, but looked away.

"I know one," she stated.

"Go on."

"A bloke goes into the doctor's and says: 'Doctor, I'm all confused. Sometimes I feel like a wigwam and sometimes I feel like a teepee." Pause. "And the doctor says: 'The trouble with you is that you're too tense."

Kevin groaned humorously.

He felt light and easy, much as he had when he had wanted to jump the canal.

Suddenly he strode forth and jumped up near the trunk of a tree to one of its branches. There he swung.

Helen's surprise was evident.

"What are you doing?" was all she could muster.

"Swinging."

She checked the path. Nobody was in sight. He'd already taken a look around. Then she stood there, completely at a loss as to what to say or do.

Still swinging, he came to her rescue.

"I really like this tree."

The branches swayed with his weight and the narrow, pointed leaves rattled.

"It's a weeping willow," she said.

"Aha."

"Come down."

He had an urge to climb and show off, but he suppressed it. He knew he was embarrassing her. Yet another difference between them.

However, he would not readily submit to her.

"What's the matter," he laughed, hanging by one arm, "don't you like me monkeying around?"

Then he dropped to his feet.

"You're quite incorrigible," she remarked.

He didn't know what it meant, but he laughed all the

same.

"You mean I need a check-up from the neck up?"

She laughed. "Something like that."

"You know a lot about nature, then?" he asked, wanting her to do the talking.

"A little."

"Go on, what's that?" he asked as they walked on, pointing to a cluster of flowers near the waterside. They grew in bunches of tiny, creamy white from numerous branches on the upper half of the main stalk. Lower down the stalk the branches carried serrated leaves.

"That's meadowsweet."

"Ho! Ho! You do know."

"Yes, and those further over, over there on the far side, see them? They're bulrushes -"

"Yes, I know those."

She continued to point to the far side of the canal.

"Over there is a sycamore and I think that's an ash. And way back there, see that one, with the acorns? That's an oak.

She was a wonderful girl. Full of knowledge. It would be nice to go out with her. A proper romance. Could he handle it? Would it be too soft and tame for him? Did she have the real spunk he liked in women?

Deep down he felt it couldn't work. She was alien to his nature. This, in itself, was attracting. He'd try. Yes, he'd try. And if he were to be disappointed, then in a perverse way he'd be relieved.

"Like us," she had said. "We'll just be friends."

"'ave you got anywhere yet?" asked Tony.

"Fuck off."

The turning for the metal bridge was in sight.

"There's some ragwort," she went on, nodding at the

clumps of yellow flowers.

"You got all this from your walks with your parents?"

"Mostly."

Kevin was interested, but he knew he would remember very little. He was brim with gen on valves, universal joints, bolts, nuts, washers, hoses, wires, rods and all manner of things. Ninety-nine times out of a hundred he could guess the correct socket or spanner for a nut or bolt whether imperial or metric.

A silence followed. Had she sensed something? He felt that his enquiry might have curtailed her. This had not been his intention and he grew awkward in the silence. He had to get her interest.

"I haven't finished the poetry book. I'll tell you what I think about it when I'm finished. You want to give me something else?"

"What would you like?"

"I don't know. Not the wandering nobody, wandering nowhere stuff. Something with a bit of nature. Set in the country."

"Thomas Hardy?"

"Okay."

"Hmmm," she mused, "he may be a bit too much. What I mean is that I find him a little heavy going."

She thought for a moment.

"What about D.H. Lawrence?"

"Isn't he supposed to be dirty?"

"No," she smiled. "He's just sensitive."

"I've seen some of the films."

"I think you'll get more out of the books... I'll give you short stories. See what you think."

What would the lads say if they could see him reading D.H. Lawrence?

"Intellectual masturbation," Tony had once remarked about something similar.

Sod 'em, he thought.

With Helen he felt he was progressing. Something he had not felt in years and it made him realise he had been drifting. Maybe he could get her down to the club? Then he'd show her how he could dance. That was his world. He'd show her he was no brickie. And he could dress. Perhaps she'd drink a little more? He'd take it slowly, real slowly. He'd been taking it slowly this far, to the extent that he'd been getting some stick from the boys. Why the hell had he told them he was seeing a barmaid? How the hell could he introduce her to them? "Scored yet?" Shit.

Tony had bumped into them in town and what a mess that had been. No, she was a flower and they would crush her. He, himself, was clumsy enough. It'd be awkward and embarrassing. They'd accept her, but they would not take her in. She wouldn't fit. And what was worse was she'd know it.

There was nothing for it, he'd have to be selective or he'd have to give her up. But to give her up would be to fall back into the mud and drifting. Screwing with Beryl and Rita. Screwing himself. He wanted to be out of the rat race. He wanted the merry-go-round to stop.

With Sandra he had progressed. Towards the end it had been bad. Fissures had opened up between them. Their conversations had been full of barbs. He had chosen broadsword and she mace, and there, they'd pummelled each other's soft defences. Hacked at their relationship. How horrible it had been in the end.

They turned right and crossed the narrow metal bridge.

The sun was lower now and although the light

through the foliage was as brilliant as before the warmth had all but disappeared. Under the canopy of trees the air was chilled.

On impulse he left the path and reached over into the green jungle and pulled out a scarlet poppy. As he did so his forearm brushed the hairs on the stem of a stinging nettle. His skin smarted with sweet pain.

Kevin presented her with the flower.

"For you."

"Thank you, Kevin," she smiled.

Ha! Only if the lads could see him now.

He rubbed his forearm, but found no relief in doing so.

"Did you get stung?"

"Yes. It's nothing really." It burnt like acid.

"Come here," she said, taking his hand and leading him back to the stinging nettles.

"What are you doing?"

"You'll see." And she let go of his hand and leant into the mass of green and flowers. From there she tore a large leaf from - what he considered - a weed.

"This is a dock leaf," she explained. "Here, hold this." He took the poppy. "It usually grows where the stinging nettles grow and -" she took him by the hand again. He felt an electricity ripple from the point of her touch "- if you rub it into where you've been stung, it neutralises the pain." She pressed and rubbed the leaf into his arm.

Kevin felt both impotent and enchanted. He looked about. No one was in sight.

"Over there, a bit more," he said, pointing with the poppy. And there she rubbed.

"Okay?" she smiled, endearingly. Her entire face smiled. Sunshine again.

"Yes."

Unable to control himself and at that moment totally besotted by her, he kissed her quickly on the lips.

Her reaction was to smile awkwardly, her eyes smoky with embarrassment, despair, pain, joy or bliss? He could not tell. Therefore he became embarrassed and then annoyed.

She dropped her eyes and he writhed with pain. He had an urge to apologise. But what for? Damn it, he would not. It was not him to do such a thing.

In agony he searched for something to say.

"It feels better now."

She nodded and carefully let go of him. Still she averted her eyes.

"Good," she replied.

Her movements were painfully slow.

"Here," he offered the poppy, struggling in anguish.

"Thanks," she smiled, dropping the leaf, taking the poppy and glancing into his eyes. There was shame in her face. Was she ashamed of her reaction? Or was there shame because she felt it wrong?

He smiled back and looked away.

"Look at those clouds over there. It looks like it might rain later."

"Yes, it does."

Was it worth wasting his time on her?

Glorious life

I'm lost to your intoxicating love,
Oh, let me breathe,
Give me some room - I'm gasping.
Slow down, I can't keep this pace

Let me stand back and look at myself,
I'll preserve this image, especially this image.
You look so much younger, almost childish.

Laughing naked demons dance around us,
They're joyous in a spiteful way.
Dancing sharp shadows,
Frantic, but there should be no hurry.
Ultimate speech, no holds barred
Are you enjoying this asphyxiation as much as me?

Happiness without laughter
Photograph this rare image
Note the expression, the forced position,
Every single murmur, slight twitch,
And the global noise.
Many all around, our expression is not rare,
But it is ours for all our lives.
Animalism is outside, but inside too.
Universally we are common,
A small pearl in an ocean of black velvet,
Soft and splashed with glitter,
But look closer, they are pearls too,
Some have our light, a star, a sun.
A volume of time and space,
Within us, without us.

He asked her whether she'd been to a certain pub.
She replied that she had not. From there he went on to talk
about how the place got round the licensing laws by serving
hot potatoes to the patrons. Everyone paid a pittance to get
in. They were given a raffle ticket, which entitled them to a
jacketed potato with a choice of toppings. In this way, under

the guise of a club, the bar stayed open until one in the morning. Sometimes a disco would be playing. Of course the place was poky, the atmosphere sleazy, yes it was a real dive, a hole, but that was the beauty of it. It was brim with characters. Some real cases.

Kevin said he would take her there and she said she'd love to go. However, he had made it sound quite romantic and she was being inquisitive, if nothing else. He wondered whether he'd overdone it. He'd not mentioned the occasional fight, the heavily made-up slags, the petty pushers... Well, if it looked as if it were to happen, he'd mention some of these things.

He was, of course, coasting. Waffling. Running from what had happened. Yet, he refused to be shaken. And this refusal shook him. Was that it? Would he give up on her now? Was there something about her he did not know? Did she harbour a secret that had made him miss time his approach? Had she bewitched him?

He fought these thoughts, throwing them aside as they came at him. He needed more distraction, more conversation. Anything. A song. He needed a tune.

Why was he so anxious? It was so unlike him. He was usually in control, more confident. It normally took a lot to shake him off once he'd put his mind to something. Yes, he was like a dog with a rag when he got something fixed in his head. He knew that -

"Kevin," she began suddenly, "I don't want -"

"Don't worry," he interrupted. "It's okay."

"I'm not sure I want anyone yet," Helen went on, regardless. "It's nothing against you."

He was irritated by the conversation. It was out of his control. And in some inexplicable way she was breaking up before him.

"Can't we take a break?" Sandra had asked.

"What do you mean?" he returned.

"Can't we not see each other for a few weeks?" she said painfully.

"Why? What's wrong? You shouldn't feel like that."

"I just want time."

"What do you mean?"

"Stop saying that!" she said angrily.

"Well I don't understand. If you want a few weeks what, what -" He was shouting now, unable to find his words. "What's the point? You don't want to go out with me any more!"

"I do. I just want time out." She was crying.

"But you shouldn't feel like that." It was totally incomprehensible to him. "Time out from what? You want me, don't you? I mean, you love me, don't you?"

"Yes." The tears were flowing freely. "Oh, I don't know. I don't know anything any more."

"Look," he began calmly, "if you want your freedom you can have it." He paused. "But you take it totally."

"No, Kevin," she managed.

He was hostile and vicious.

"It's Matthew, isn't it?" he ventured.

She said nothing.

"Isn't it?"

"Nothing's happened."

"You want something to happen?"

Again she said nothing.

"Well?"

"I don't know."

"Yes, you do."

"Kevin, don't."

"Don't what?"

"Just don't."
Pause.
"You do want something to happen."
"Okay, yes. Is that what you want to hear?"
"Fine. Bloody fine." He was tumbling. "Well go ahead. Take it. Do what the fuck you want!"
"But I don't know. Don't you see?"
"All I see is that you don't want me."
"Kevin," she pleaded. "I don't know what I want."
"Fine. Well, I'm making the decision for you."
She was silent, her eyes cast downwards.
"Okay?"
Then she nodded.

Fears

I feel like flying from this claustrophobic warmth,
I want to take a time trip to deliver me from life,
And here come those fears again, they've been waiting
Like the avenger in the shadows clasping the cold knife.

Have you heard?
They've given honorary life membership to the traffic warden killed,
And they're recycling all the war's blood, that was spilled;
They've got a safe transplant for all the hearts filled,
And Henry Kissinger's links say they have the waters stilled.

I love to hear the tiger licking
At the frothing rabies between your legs.
Warming you in the blooded cup of my hands.
Eating us up, drinking the dregs.
Hey, the nuclear program is smouldering in the laboratory

And a pyromaniac has burnt the Government White Paper.
They say discrimination can be ended
And that's Batman's new caper!

I'm whimpering under the weight of your love,
And the inflation that has hit cheap entertainment.
I'm screaming at all the apathy
Like a political lobby that only echoes lament.
And our collared leprechauns warrant an apology.
Hey, street urchin: when are you going home?
And here come those fears again, they've been waiting
Like the hooligan with the sharpened steel comb!

Schools of fish and mathematics have gone comprehensive
And swarms of ants are chewing New York,
Our gyrating love can power a nuclear station
And thought manipulation can make the pig talk.
The view from this cliff-top is tremendous
Because without crampons, sunglasses and ice-axe,
And through the glare of the sun
I can see children eaten, by wolves in ice packs.
They've trapped fear in a wardrobe
And themselves in mind's disease,
They're descending on all the disillusioned
Snapping and sucking like clouds of fleas.
The candle flickers as the stars explode,
The clouds fall and the sun fades,
And love bends light
As the alien invades.
It's no longer real,
Night no longer divides day,
And I cannot feel,
The words you say.

And you're a man in a damp street,
You're a man with the snakes at his feet
You're the news recorded on a sheet,
You're dripping, just hanging meat.
Oh lover, you're too close
Oh lover, you're too far
No lover, you're a skull
Go away lover you're a scar.
And my mind is blown
My love is stone
My body is bone
I stand alone.

"Let's just take it as it comes," Kevin said, as they came out onto the common once again.

"Okay," agreed Helen.

The dirty, slate-coloured clouds dominated the horizon. Their awesome silent anger made the couple feel quite vulnerable and small in the field.

In the distance the kids were still playing football and seemed oblivious to the impending storm. The barbecue party, however, had begun to pack away.

Characteristically he rose up with renewed vigour, ignoring the incident.

"I'm glad I changed my mind about the shopping... And you're going to stay in and do some work?"

"Yes. I won't get it done next weekend; being at home and all."

"Yeah."

"Do you see your Mum often?"

"Naw, not really I suppose. Once every three or four months. That's good for me. I used to go home about twice a year at most. I'd lived away from home so long that it was a real trip in the past. Things have changed, but it's still a strange feeling."

"I think everyone feels that."

Huh, she was so warm to him now.

"I guess so. Perhaps I'm a little selfish."

"We're all guilty of that to some extent."

Kevin wanted to laugh at this comment but thought better of it. Because of this, he lost the thread of the conversation and another silence fell upon them.

The distant houses and the alleyway to the main road seemed to be getting no closer. Whereas the billowing overhead sea was almost upon them. The day was rapidly losing its charm.

"We'd better step it up a bit, otherwise we're going to get drenched."

She nodded a reply.

A cold wind caused her to cross her arms upon herself.

"Earlier I'd wished I'd worn shorts. Now I wished I'd brought an umbrella."

She smiled.

"I was thinking of doing some of my work in the garden. Some of the sketches." She paused. "In my bikini."

At this he would have made some flirtatious remark, had he not been subdued.

"I'm still going weight-training."

"To get rid of your enormous belly," she joked.

He smiled. No pain, no strain, no gain.

"We don't seem to be getting any closer. I'm sure there's something funny about this common."

"It's pretty big."

"I've run round it a couple of times. It's a bit boring though."

"I find running boring, full stop."

"Hmmm," he agreed. "It gives you time to think."

"I do that in the bath."

Again he suppressed a saucy remark.

In places the clouds were as dark as the matt, blue-grey of the tiles of the houses before them. Red brick and sandstone alike were rendered drab by the oppressive overcast. The sounds of the traffic - now in earshot - were flattened, as if one complex machine made the noises. An avenue of traffic dwarfed and trapped, contrasting the easy flow of the monster overhead.

Helen led them, as she had on the way to the pub, into the alley. Here, the unnatural darkness held a bitterly severe chill. Sinister. Before them the cars and lorries, hissing, sighing, protesting and roaring. Behind them the uncaring expanse of shelterless ground. And above, the devouring silent onslaught of cloud.

If Kevin had been alone he would have run. Not merely to save himself from the imminent rain, but to warm himself up.

They were out of the alleyway, hastening along the roadside. All colour and vibrancy had evaporated. The press of the sky took the light out of the colours and dropped everything into bland shade. Dullness filmed everything, lifting the dirt and stains. And of the few people on the pavement, those wearing loud colours looked stupid.

Kevin looked to Helen and saw that her features were harsher than before. The line of her nose was hard, the angle of her eyebrows - without a frown - were set in a kind of quizzical distemper. Her entire appearance, like her gait, was no longer relaxed.

Kevin felt like saying something, but like her he too wanted to get inside, and to talk, in some strange way, was to prolong their exposure to the elements.

He looked to the long line of traffic; saw the tensed or relaxed, pissed off faces. And he smiled in empathy. And his mood changed. So what if it rained? So what if you got held up a little while? He knew that in the drivers he had seen himself; but it was this very fact that caused him to smile.

He turned to Helen to share his discovery and amusement, but was held off by her appearance. He then realised it was something he could not share. She would not understand and he could not explain. He would only succeed in estranging himself.

"It's going to be a corker when it starts," he found himself saying.

"Yes. I can't wait to get in."

"Almost there."

They were virtually shouting above the din of the traffic, the occasional horn and distant roadwork - the cause for the increased congestion. Because of this they fell silent again.

Then they were at her front door.

"Thanks for a lovely day, Kevin," she said, having retrieved her key from her purse.

"Thank you," he returned, smiling.

Pause.

"I'll, er, give you a ring during the week. P'haps a quiet drink, eh?"

"Yes, that'll be nice. It'll probably only be a quick one because of my work."

"Fine," he said, not wanting to hear any more. Could he walk off without giving her a kiss? Brinkmanship. He knew the name of the game.

"Thanks for this," she said, holding up the poppy.

"My pleasure," he nodded.

Silence. Deuce?

"You can come in, if you like."

"No, that's okay." Cool. "Thanks anyway." One up.

Had it been a genuine offer?

She turned to her door and he began to shuffle about on his toes, as much from impatience as from the cold.

"So, I'll hear from you, then? Make it Wednesday or Thursday," she said when she was in the hallway.

"Yeah, okay." He wouldn't give her a proper kiss. No, not after the earlier fiasco. "If I can't make it, I'll still phone you." He had to retain his individuality.

She nodded.

Ah, hell.

He leaned in the doorway and she moved forward. A pleasant peck of a kiss, on the lips, passed between them.

They smiled and he stepped back half-turning.

"See you," she said.

"Bye."

Then, a little awkwardly, he turned to the road and he heard the door click shut behind him.

Damn, he thought. His anger rose up with such swiftness that he was taken unawares. Had he kept it at bay so successfully that he had not been aware of its magnitude? The word had automatically snapped in his mind. Like a reflex. Had he been alone behind closed doors he may have said it aloud.

"She's got y' by the short'n'curlies."

"Fuck off and die."

Why was he angry? He put it down to the parting kiss. A feeble effort. But he knew it was more than that. It had been a culmination of events. A slow attrition of his "winning her over" offensive. Not only today, but every time he had taken her out.

He weaved his way across the nervous flow of traffic and went briskly up the hill.

After all these weeks he felt he had made little or no progress. Admittedly, he'd only seen her four times, but nevertheless he felt he was dragging his feet. It was getting him down. Was she really worth it?

She had been radiant.

"Same again?"

"Please." Then, "thank you Kevin."

The voicing of his name had touched him. And yes, he could have leapt the canal for her. Had she somehow bewitched him?

She was worth it, but did she care for him?

"We'll just be friends," she had said.

Did she truly believe that? Damn it, of course she did. But people change. They come round. Did he have the required energy?

Kevin returned to his initial question. Was she really worth it?

This was ridiculous. Was he going soft or something?

He forced himself to think of something else.

What would he do when he got back? Shopping was definitely out. Perhaps write that letter to his aunt? He always put that off... Check out the afternoon sport and film? Get ready for weight training. Yes, there was plenty to do.

"Make it Wednesday or Thursday," she had requested.

Ha, who was she, dictating to him?

Much as he tried he could not keep his thoughts from returning to her.

After leaving her, his exclamation, the word damn,

had signalled the opening of the floodgates. Not literally. But such was his frustration.

He seemed to be trying to scale the unscalable.

A strong wind rose up and pushed at him. The clouds raced, tumbling and surging over one another.

The small park was deserted. A lonely space, empty and abandoned. And as he climbed, the noise of the traffic receded, adding to the eerie calm.

He forced his mind to focus on the sensation of Now he had experienced whilst looking at the play of light on the small sandstone cottage wall. It was an enigma. He could not explain the sensation. He could not pinpoint its source. Equally puzzling, he could not recapture it. Not even a morsel. It was gone. He viewed it coldly, trying to dissect it. And so it was cold.

Only if one could live all their life in such clarity.

Kevin had turned into his street when he noticed the spots of dark on the pale grey pavement. Large drops of rain fell intermittently. He felt them individually and distinctly. He began to jog. It was just as he did so, that like the opening of a trap door, the heavens bucketed down. He broke into a sprint, but by the time he had reached his front door he was soaked.

He closed the main door behind him and as he went to the entrance to his flat he thought of meeting the lads later.

"'ave you got anywhere yet?" Tony had persisted.

Ah, it was none of their business. Nosy bleeders.

At his door he dug for his key as he shuffled his feet on the brush mat with the branded black legend: Wipe your feet stupid.

He opened his flat door and was swept over by a sudden depression. It was exactly as he'd left it all those light-years ago. But more lifeless and dull for the darkness outside. No noise, no life, save the tap of the rain upon the windows, rising now and then with the wind.

He went straight to the television to fill the place with some semblance of life. Then pulling off his sodden T-shirt he entered the bathroom. There he furiously rubbed his hair with a towel. When he'd finished he threw both the towel and the T-shirt into the wickerwork wash-basket.

From the lounge he heard the commentator's voice racing with the horses. In the bathroom it sounded like garbled nonsense.

Kevin viewed himself in the mirror. A spot of grit just below the left eye. Carefully he brought up a finger and rolled it away. It was then that he noticed his callused hands and dirty fingernails. The depression took a firmer hold.

"Fuck," he exclaimed. This was how he appeared to her. Well, sod her. He could do better.

Ah, he was being stupid. A real pleb. He'd take out his frustration later, through weight training.

He tensed his stomach and swung a clenched fist into it.

"Ahhh," he yelped. Pain, from his bruise, flared up and a dull throb began as he inspected it. "You're a fuckin' idiot Kev," he said aloud.

He was sitting in the chair. The bleeding wouldn't stop. The wad of tissues he held at his calf was almost completely saturated. Only the corners were still snow white.

"How'd it happen?" asked Mick, coming noisily down the wooden steps, Greasy following.

All the work in the garage had come to a virtual standstill. Only the radio continued.

"It's nofin' Mick," said Kevin. It did not hurt so

much; a sort of needle-like pain, sharp but localised. As far as he was concerned it looked worse than it felt. So much blood.

Mick was humourless. "That wasn't what I asked."

Martin, who'd been standing over Kevin, piped up.

"We were getting that exhaust off that bastard there - " and he pointed to an elevated vehicle in front of them. "It was a stubborn sucker. We were pulling at it when it suddenly snapped. It swung down Kevin's end and hit him in the leg."

"Let's have a look," said Mick.

Kevin exposed the gash.

"Hospital," said Mick.

"What?" protested Kevin. Surely a quick bandage would put everything in order?

"Martin, take him in the Volvo."

"Sure," said Martin, pleased as Punch with the chance to skive legitimately.

"But -" Kevin began.

"No buts Kevin. That thing's rusty. Get a tetanus jab." He left before anything more could be said, returning to his overhead office.

Kevin removed his shoes and took a sweatshirt from his wardrobe in the bedroom. Outside was quite mean and he felt cold because of it.

Back in the lounge he switched the television channels and came to some old black and white movie on BBC2.

After the company and brightness of the day he felt lonely and low. In the kitchen the kettle was filled and switched on.

Anger pulled down his brow as he tea-spooned coffee granules into a mug. He knew what to do.

He silenced the television so that the story lost some meaning and became a series of pictures.

Fingering the albums he pulled out one by Leonard Cohen. Balancing the vinyl on one spread-eagled hand, careful not to touch the surface, he made ready the stereo with the other.

He could never explain why he did not find this melancholic artist depressing. Maybe it was that the artist's music itself was so depressing that it uplifted him? A case of "it could be worse"?

Sandra had introduced him to this solo-guitarist with the monotonous voice. A distinct sound of his own, they had followed him in cult-like fashion. Kevin found something in the unique sound. A restful solace. A soulful kind of giving-up. He could not say what it was. However, it was this personal appreciation that allowed him to play it. Occasionally it reminded him of Sandra - they had had *their* songs - but overall it did not.

The kettle clicked off as the hiss, pop and crackle of this particular, well-worn record filled the room.

He was pouring the hot water into the mug when the flash occurred. He counted. The long roll of thunder came sometime later.

"Quite far away," he said to himself, and he looked through his kitchen window at the out-of-focus buildings.

He brought the mug to his lips and warmed his face on the hot vapours. Leonard Cohen's heavy, masculine voice sang of deep passionate love and deep passionate hate whilst his acoustic guitar bounced tunefully along. Such a contrast of music and lyrics. Almost a contradiction.

The buildings beyond the kitchen rippled and buckled through the wash of the window. Kevin stood there for a while, the coffee too hot to drink, absorbed by the hard edges becoming fluid.

Then he abruptly turned, as if it had not been his will to do so, walked into the lounge and with the mug on the floor slumped onto the sofa.

He watched the television with no interest whatsoever and he yawned. It was a long satisfying yawn and it made him realise that he hadn't had much sleep. But he didn't want to sleep, so he took up the challenge of figuring out the plot of the film, the goodies and baddies, without the aid of the dialogue.

Almost unconsciously the film took him in. He was not so much interested in the plot as to confirming his suspicions as to what was going on. Therefore, he rose and turned the volume up, but left the stereo alone.

The film was third-rate and he kept telling himself to turn it off, but lethargy had taken him and he remained slumped and dull-eyed. Eventually the conflict of sound moved him from his slumber. Once again the volume was turned off on the television.

When he sat back again he found his lids heavy. Still he resisted the urge to sleep. He'd done nothing all day - nothing productive that is - and he felt guilty for it.

Kevin sipped his coffee.

Plan of attack, he thought. He'd write the letter to get his brain ticking over, then he'd go weight-training. Hopefully it would have stopped raining by then.

He rose from the sofa and collecting pen and paper from a drawer he sat at the table; his coffee at his elbow.

"Dear Aunty," he began. "Sorry for not writing sooner. There's no excuses."

Were there excuses? No. People did what they wanted. And he found letter writing a chore.

He sat the table, his chin in one hand, a pen in the

other and stared first at the television and then out of the window.

The storm outside emphasised a sort of cosiness in being inside. The drone of Leonard Cohen began to burden him. He knew he was being seduced by sleep again.

Why was he so tired? He then worked out exactly how much sleep he had had last night. Yes, he was justified in having a little kip. So let sleep take him. He felt happy in himself. The conflict was over.

Kevin got up - feeling a twinge of guilt for putting off the letter again - turned the stereo to the radio and curled up on the sofa.

Sleep did not come to him immediately and he lay staring blankly at the television.

"I guess that makes me brown, then," he laughed.

"Oh no," she exclaimed. "You're more red or orange."

"Reddish brown?"

"No, you've got orange. Happy and easy."

People were complicated. Yes, he was happy and easy. But he was also angry and moody. Rebel without applause. She didn't know him. Know him fully. That takes time, a lot of time, sometimes a lifetime. He was not sure he knew himself fully.

"It's not a film. There needn't be a happy ending. Or a proper ending."

At this moment he felt he had stopped. Things were moving along. But he was not progressing. He was not going anywhere. It was as if he was waiting. Waiting for what? A kick up the arse? He wasn't sure. He wouldn't mind waiting if he knew what he was waiting for. Occasionally, these days, he felt profoundly bored.

No, Helen did not know him.

"Don't pull hard on my ties," he said.

"Okay," she smiled, wickedness sparkling in her eyes.

He knotted the stockings about her ankles and the bed's frame. Her wrists were secured more loosely with two of his thin ties.

Sandra was prostrate and totally naked before him.

"Right," he clapped his hands together loudly. "Now you're mine. I can do anything I want."

Her smile was slightly askew, but her eyes shone with delight.

He jumped on the bed between her spread legs. She flinched.

"Take your underpants off," she said softly.

"Make me," he laughed, sitting upon his folded legs.

"Now," he walked up one of her shins with two fingers, each miniature step separated by a word. "What -" step "- shall -" step "- we -" step "- do -" step "- with -" step "- you?" He was at the top of her thigh. She was hushed with expectation.

Kevin lifted the same hand and ran a finger lightly down her front, circling her belly button and then rising up to circle each of her nipples.

She closed her eyes.

Carefully he rose upward so that he was over her on all fours. She opened her eyes and peaked at him.

"Take them off," she whispered thickly.

He smiled and put on the most evil face he could find. Then he lowered his face to hers to kiss her.

"No," and she snapped her head to the side. "Take them off first."

He pushed his tongue into her ear. She struggled, but it was more a squirm. He pushed himself off her and she turned her face to him. Eyes wide and full of excitement.

She parted her lips and a sliver of tongue teased him.

He smiled and descended for the kiss. Just at the last moment she again turned her head away.

"You've had it now," he threatened.

"Ppphuhh," was her response.

He pushed himself away and crouched to one side of her.

When he made no movement, she looked at him and as she did so, he began looking about the room.

"Where's that broom?" he asked himself.

She laughed.

"Oooh, yes please," she said.

"Slag," he accused.

"Bastard," she returned.

And they laughed.

Carefully, he lay alongside her, leaning on an elbow, one of his legs crossing one of hers. Then with his free hand he delicately tweaked her nipples.

Kevin loved to watch them harden under his play. He kissed them and then caressed them with his tongue, cupping the far breast with a palm.

Sandra's eyes were closed. She was completely motionless.

He sat up and let his hands wander over her. They explored the feel of her.

Slowly he concentrated one hand on the inside of her thighs, whilst the other meandered over her face, neck and breasts. Every time his hand came near her mouth she invited his fingers with her tongue. He smiled, but did not linger to accept the invitations.

In the meantime his other hand could feel her thighs quivering minutely, as he excited certain areas. He moved close to her mound, at the sides, near the edge, and he felt her shift ever so slightly for him to touch her. But still he did not.

By now his erection was painful in his underwear, but he did not want to break the flow he'd set up in her.

She whispered something.

"What?" he enquired in a dreamlike voice.

"Take them off."

Maintaining the play at the tops of her legs he awkwardly removed his underpants. His penis sprung out and he was relieved.

Sandra looked down at him and smiled.

Then Kevin touched her with his fingers and she froze.

"Blimey," he whispered, " you're so wet."

After a few moments using his fingers he shifted his position and used his tongue.

Gradually she was swept away by his touch until she was writhing and pulling at her bindings. Side to side, up and down; she was totally transported.

Then she began moaning and Kevin felt himself losing control. So he broke the rhythm and came away, delicately crawling up her body with his tongue.

She was waiting, no, yearning for him when he entered her, just as she was waiting for his tongue to wrestle with hers.

"I just want to open my legs wider and wider for you."

When he awoke it was pitch black and still raining outside.

"Shit," he cursed aloud, when he saw the time.

The glow of the television picture played games in shadow with the room. The stereo had slipped the station and irritatingly crackled up and down in volume.

Weight training was a no-no. It had gone half-past six. Freddy would have to get someone else to spot for him.

"Breathe out for effort, Kev."

Also he had not telephoned Ian and he hadn't started his dinner. He'd have to be out at a quarter to nine at the latest.

He got up brusquely and corrected the radio setting - the top twenty was playing. He switched on the standing lamp, drew the curtains and turned off the television.

"Holy shit, don't pop yer balls, mate." He smiled at this. It was what he'd said to Freddy, who'd almost dropped the bar. Of course it'd been a stupid thing to do, but Kevin had been spotting him. No sweat. Kevin went for repetition rather than weight. He wanted lean muscles and not the bulbous things Freddy sported. Each to his own.

A cup of cold black coffee sat beside the beginnings of a letter. He picked up the mug and drank it down in one go. Then he exhaled loudly to ride the shock of the bitter, icy mixture.

On went the light in the kitchen and on went the kettle. He lined up three dirty potatoes and searched for the spud-peeler.

Thus, the cooking was under way.

Pork chop, mash and frozen veg. Just like a Sunday, he thought.

And he felt it could be Sunday. His late afternoon nap had mucked up his internal clock. Was it only today he'd gone to the pub with Helen? It seemed like yesterday, or even a week ago.

When the food was cooking he called Ian. Yes, nine to nine-thirty at the usual. The lads had agreed. They weren't going on to the club. Lack of funds.

"Hope Terry let's you in," Ian had said.

After the telephone conversation Kevin shifted the sofa and cleared other things from the centre of the room.

So, he wouldn't get down to the centre. Well, he'd at least have a quick workout.

He began with a few basic stretching exercises. Press-ups and sit-ups followed these. Out for effort. Then he fetched his skipping rope from his kit bag in the bedroom and began.

Kevin felt good. Tiredness and boredom fell from him in great lumps; like lumps of lead. His body, working up a reasonable sweat, let all the stiffness slip off. With it his worries seemed to go. And then his frustrations. His mind focused. His energies, mounting by the second; channelled.

Quickly, he pulled off his socks, sweatshirt and jeans. Then he started up again.

"Like us," she had said. "We'll just be friends." Ha, that's what you think missy.

"You and who's army?" He felt like laughing.

Ah, it was great to be alive. The cold in the room was dispelled. The drawn curtains encapsulated his warmth. He was awake. Marvellously awake. His mind clear. His body fluid, loose and firm at the same time.

He could be in the weight-training room, hypnotically pumping the equipment; mechanised. The Rocky theme played in his ears followed by Survivor's *Eye of the Tiger*, another favourite at the centre.

He stopped and ran in to check the food.

"Damn," he cursed, as he burnt his fingers trying to turn the chop over in the grill pan. He flicked on the kettle.

The kitchen lino was cold to his bare feet and although the food was almost ready - the chop overdone on one side - he returned to the lounge and dressed.

He rushed around and everything flowed. He was

bursting with energy. Off with the stereo and on with the television. Table and chair manoeuvred for viewing. Back in the kitchen: knife, fork and plate out. Two slices of bread, margarined and ready. Boiled water from the kettle into the pan, salted and hob position lit up. Out with the frozen vegetables and into the pan. Boiled potatoes off and water drained away. Salt, pepper, margarine, and milk mashed in - peel and all - with a fork. Mash: good stomach liner for a session. Vegetables down to a simmer. Almost ready.

As he sat at the table with his meal he experienced a great feeling of well-being. A contentment rather than a passionate uplifting.

It was good to be alive. He had his health, his own flat and a job. It could be much worse. Of course he moaned. Everyone moaned. It was a national pastime. Anyway, was anyone ever totally satisfied? Certainly not in his circle of friends. Some days work was a bitch. Some days he wished for a cleaner job. But he knew he'd go potty behind a desk. But to try something different. To break out. Maybe his true vocation was out there somewhere. Opportunity would never knock. What else could he do? He'd never know. Ah, for the opportunity to try something else. Experience. But he was tied by responsibility. The responsibility of the flat. The responsibility of maintaining a norm in society. His slot. That was it. His slot. He couldn't drop out for a time and get back in if he didn't like it. That was for the rich. If he dropped out, tried something different, he'd be ostracised. Cast out by the people of his station as a weirdo. Or at best somebody who thought himself above them. Yes, he'd be ostracised. Or was it that he simply didn't have the bottle? Kevin felt that if he had more behind him: money, status, he'd have the bottle. To have bottle you had to be crazy or have the backing of some clout. Perhaps if he'd gone further in his schooling he'd have had the luxury of choice. Choice was what he wanted. But no, he was tied to the treadmill as surely as if he were chained to a millstone or the oar of a galley.

He glanced at the writing pad as he ate.

"Dear Aunty,

Sorry for not writing sooner. There's no excuses."

Should that be: "There're no excuses."? He wasn't sure. Shit it.

"When are you coming over for good?" his aunty had asked.

"I don't know. Soon, but I still want to see a bit more of Europe first."

Then his father had died. His mother had said: "go your own way. I don't need looking after." But he'd bought the flat and decided to stick around for a time. Of course the mortgage was a burden. He found the repayments strangled him. But he had no regrets on that score. It was still cheaper than renting.

Would he ever get away? Did he really want to get away? Get away? Get away from what?

Things weren't so bad. He was middling.

After the meal, piling the dishes and pans in the kitchen sink, he went to the bathroom, took off his sweatshirt and had a good wash.

He felt low again. But not like before. He didn't care so much. The weekend was almost over. Sunday tomorrow. He was out tonight and didn't really feel like the heavy session it promised to be. But it was go out or stay in. And staying in meant moping. He'd not finished the letter - ha, he'd hardly started it - and he didn't feel like doing it. Finally, he'd not resolved his relationship with Helen one way or the other.

In about half an hour he'd have to leave.

Damn it. Damn it all! He'd have to get some music on. Blast everything away.

So he went into the lounge, turned off the television and took out The Clash's first album and turned on the stereo. The radio came on and interrupted his setting up of the record. He left it and obeyed David Bowie's chant to *Let's Dance*.

Kevin moved this way and that and slowly worked himself out of the depression.

What did anything matter?

With the single over he turned on the record and allowed The Clash to put violence in the air.

Kevin went to the bedroom and took a look in the wardrobe for suitable clothing. To fit his mood. He pulled out a white shirt and a thin black leather tie.

This was one of the ties that had been used for a purpose for which it had not been designed. They'd had to cut her stockings free!

He was stripped to the waist. Looking into the long mirror he accompanied the music with aggressive faces: pulling his eyebrows down, thinning his lips, flaring his eyes, tilting his head.

Then he jumped back and raised his fists like a boxer. He eyed his biceps.

"You and whose fucking army?"

"Kiss my arse."

"You're cruisin' for a bruisin', matey."

"Here's a knuckle sandwich. Chew on that!"

And he boxed the air, at first precisely and cleverly like a boxer, ducking this way and that, then violently, in a frenzied blur of movement. His heart beat like mad and he panted.

"Come on!" he shouted.

The music spurred him on.

When he stopped, he blew himself up in front of the mirror like an aggressive piranha. He tensed his entire body and enjoyed the cut of muscle.

After the roll-on deodorant he donned his white shirt, pushing its tails into his jeans. On with his training shoes and then into the kitchen for a drink of water.

He was frustrated by the difficulty of getting the glass under the tap. The awkward structure of dishes and pans rose up out of the plastic bowl in the sink to hinder him.

The darkness outside was sinister. The light from the kitchen shrunk from the blackness. It had stopped raining, but the dull objects had been darkened further by dampness and the reflective objects themselves - next door's greenhouse - looked hard and unyielding, like shells, resilient and without depth.

He returned to the bedroom and pushed a few things around. He half-heartedly tidied up, for he knew he would possibly return pissed, in which case the chaos of the room could anger or depress him. Besides, there was always the possibility of bringing someone back. There wasn't much to be done of course, folding his sweatshirt on the chair and such. He'd made the bed seemingly inviting for Helen. Helen...

The record came to an end and plunged the flat into deathly silence. Glancing at the clock and deciding that it was still too early to leave, he flipped the record over and started the B-side. He clicked his fingers and jerked his body to the music as he returned to the bedroom.

He discovered an old cup of coffee with a teaspoon in it under the chair. It was white and looked from the quantity as if it had not been touched. Obviously not one of his, he took it black. Furthermore it was on the wrong side of the bed. "Somebody else, Watson." Probably one he had made for Beryl. Rita never came here on account of the kid.

"Let's go back to your place," she'd suggested.

"Okay," he'd agreed drunkenly.

They'd walked back, arms at their sides. Separate.

Their lovemaking had been long and relaxed. Not the animal rush of the early days. They were used to each other and knew what each liked. Also, he was drunk. And drunkenness took him one way or the other. All or nothing. Both abandoned themselves to the physical, prolonging it and then sadistically killing it. Working, working, signalling and receiving, knowing when to be violent in the fight. Lies and deceit. Such an aphrodisiac. Working, hating, loving the thing, the bite. Then ripping it up, tearing it to pieces like the paper-thin relationship it was. And then coming apart, lying separately and passing through the silence first with exhaustion and then with sleep. Or sometimes entangled, falling into sleep and later, during the night, rolling apart in slumber. Whichever, they awoke separate.

It was time to go.

He put on the thin black tie, knotting it below his open-neck collar and grabbed his donkey jacket - his brother had nicked it for him from the building site on which he worked. With this over his shoulder he went in the lounge to kill the music.

However, he changed his mind when the next track began. It was one of his favourites. He threw the heavy black jacket on the sofa as the haunting, wandering guitars and thomp-thomp drums of the track began. Joe Strummer of The Clash began asking: *What's my name?*

Kevin shouted with the singer.

Then he was out, at the last minute grabbing his cheap umbrella - a pound down the market. Wearing his jacket, he hooked the umbrella handle under his armpit, concealing it, like a weapon.

He was in the aggressive mood he wanted to be. Annihilated.

Birds

Sharpened pen
Cutting the words
Scratching the paper
Killing the birds
Song and chirping
Not plagued by thought
At our level
They ought to be taught

About this devil

Trapped within
A caged cranium
It can spin
Like bottled rage

Sharpened pen
Making me bleed
Weep then
As much as you need.

A drink with the boys. He was looking forward to it. But he knew his mood was shaky. He felt it in the balance. His anger would desert him and unless he was with the boys, swept up by the laughter and bravado, he would plummet. But if he'd stayed in on a Saturday night he would only have moped. For now he ignored the flimsiness of his disposition and listened to The Clash in his head.

Nobody was out in the icy freshness of the night. An overcast sky cut out the moon. The pavement shone with yellow-orange lamplight. These smudges of brightness seemed to try to dig vertically into the pavement as if it were frozen liquid, but the gravel road allowed no such illusion and the light was merely smeared on its hard surface.

He could hear the cars from the main road at the bottom of the hill. Such was the clarity of the night air. The vehicles swished over the wet road and were only drowned by the sound of the trees and garden bushes shivering in the wind. An occasional dripping sound would come to his ears; distinct, as if issuing from a tap.

Kevin held his jacket close to him, his hands pushed into its voluminous pockets. He had pulled the shirt collar up to stop the jacket's rough surface from irritating his neck.

Briskly he walked by the park. A lone black figure in a virtually monochromatic world. A dead world that rejected him and sent him on his way.

As he passed the barren park he recalled passing it earlier that day. Then he thought of Helen. Sod her. Ah, bugger it, she was a nice girl. Too nice? Yeah, maybe too nice for him.

"I don't know how I got it," he pleaded.

Sandra frowned.

"Look, just go to the doctor's, will you?"

She nodded, looking at him suspiciously.

"I'm telling you, I've been with no one else. If you don't believe me that's your business. Boy, you're really pissing me off."

Still she remained silent.

"And if you don't believe me," he went on angrily, "it just shows you what we've got. You don't bleedin' trust me."

"I believe you. I believe you, okay?" She could see he was becoming heated enough to say something rash.

"Right," he snapped. Yes, he was angry enough to chuck her. Look at what a little pressure would reveal.

After a time he laughed in a despairing way.

She looked at him quizzically.

"You've got to laugh, haven't you? First the pregnancy and now this. We don't seem to be having much luck. Perhaps somebody's trying to tell us something."

She smiled, masking her nervousness. Then, to shield this and to stop him dwelling on the subject, she went over and hugged him.

They kissed.

At the main road he found it difficult to judge the speed of the vehicles. All he could discern were pairs of white lights and vague outlines. Colour had deserted the machines. The road itself shone like matt-black glass and allowed the lights to drop into it.

Seeing his chance he ran across, pressing the umbrella to himself. This short run put a bounce in his step.

So what if he didn't go out with Helen? What did anything matter?

He smiled.

For some reason he remembered that he'd forgotten to collect a book from her when he'd dropped her off. What was it now? Then he remembered, D.H. Lawrence.

He went on to recall the film of Lady Chatterley's Lover. It had been very physically orientated. It couldn't work today. Or could it? He could be the gamekeeper, Mellors, and Helen would be Lady Chatterley. And like

Lady Chatterley, Helen would have to be moving away from something to notice him. Ah, but it was a story and therefore contrived.

Kevin was swept over by weariness. He felt he'd done a lot and because of this he felt old.

Before this feeling became too pronounced he shunned it, filling his mind with a tune. He conjured up *Don't bang a drum* by The Waterboys.

A few figures moved about, but he did not really see them. He was isolated from them all, making his way to the pub and the company of his mates.

The grey-white wispy smoke from the exhaust of a car sitting at the lights made him think of the time when he was on his way to school. He had crossed the common in the fog and had been fascinated by the fact that he had to guess his way. But he had been especially taken by the fact that no matter how hard he looked in any direction he could not extend the circle of his vision. He could move in any direction and the fog was always the same distance ahead of him. A grey wall that rolled before him. Complete and impenetrable. Reducing clarity to his immediate surroundings.

A turn left. Over the bridge and passed the fire station he went. As he crossed the road he felt like running. His spirit was free. The wind hardened him and determination etched his face. But he didn't run.

This road was not as busy as the last and the cars swished by individually. Fixed black beings sat in the vehicles. Where were they going? Bah, who gives a shit?

He turned into a quiet side road lined with parked cars in front of terraced houses.

Kevin could see the glow of the pub ahead. Warm light through coloured glass. And as he approached the murmur of voices grew.

Drawn like a moth, he thought.

Then, perversely, something within him shrank from the warmth and light. As if he'd become a night creature. And he wanted the pub to be further away. But his legs carried him onwards and his step did not falter.

Inside, the familiarity welcomed him. Nevertheless, he rose inside himself - shields up - to the challenge of some inexplicable confrontation.

Terry was preoccupied and did not see him enter.

Kevin scanned the tables. Steve was looking straight at him, smiling. Kevin rocked his hand as if he held a sleever. In response, Steve picked up his glass, examined the contents exaggeratedly and nodded.

"Best?" Kevin mouthed, not wanting to shout.

Steve nodded and brought the sleever to his lips as Kevin found a space at the bar.

He hoped Terry would turn from the other end of the bar and see him. He didn't want to appear to be sneaking in.

The young bloke took his order. Two pints of best from the barrel. Ah, the elixir of life.

At the table Kevin took his place alongside Steve on the long padded bench against the wall.

"Thought I was late," said Kevin.

"Naw. Tony said he'd be here 'bout nine-thirty."

"Ian said he'd be early."

"Ian says a lot of things."

"Yeah."

Pause.

"Cheers," said Steve, taking up the new pint.

"Yeah."

For a moment they supped in silence.

The pub was fairly crowded. Most of the seats were taken. Plenty of standing room, though.

"How's your side?"

"Okay."

"It's a wonder Terry let you in."

"Ah, he's a good sort," said Kevin. Then, after a deliberate pause and another sup of his beer, "besides, he hasn't seen me."

Steve laughed and Kevin smiled.

"What if that fucker comes in again?" Steve wondered, after they'd set down their pints.

"He'd better be wearing chain-mail."

Steve chuckled.

"How's work?" enquired Steve, after a further drinking pause. They'd not been able to talk properly the previous evening because they'd been part of the group, and then conversation was always banter, or at least a collective thing. In addition, Steve had arrived later.

"Okay. Same old rigmarole." Then, as if he'd now thought of an answer: "Y'remember that ponce with the Volvo and the executive bum-shine. You know, the stuck up one with the crystal-cut accent who kept on telling us how to do the work. Prat." Sip. "Well, he came back on Thursday and gave the boss a bit of lip. He comes poncin' in, all blown up with his self-importance and goes up to Mick's orifice -" that's what they called Mick's office "- and starts hassling him about being overcharged. It was real up-in-arms stuff. Squawking like nobody's business. Bleedin' feathers everywhere. We could hear 'em down on the floor. 'cause you know Mick, 'e doesn't take these fings lying down." Pause for a sip. "I mean, talk about he who shouts loudest wins. You could 'ear 'em over the radio. And he knew a few words too."

Steve shook his head at the wonder of it.

"So what happened?"

"He paid."

Steve laughed and then so did Kevin.

"They're all the same," resumed Kevin. "Bloody snob. I'll tell you, mate, the more money they've got, the tighter their hold on it."

"Too right. I'll drink to that."

"You'll drink to anything."

They drank again.

"Ah, what the hell. He'll probably bust a blood vessel before he's fifty. Or have a heart attack."

Steve nodded.

"How about you?" asked Kevin.

"Okay. Smelly feet that's all I get."

"At least when you meet people you're clean."

"Yeah, like a dog's bleedin' dinner. The old man allowed us to take our jackets off today. But we had to keep our ties on, of course."

"What about that new girl?"

"What? Jayne, with the nice arse?"

"Yeah, is that he name? The new trainee from up north."

Steve smiled.

"Huh," he began. "Thought I had that cracked, but she's got some boyfriend who comes down at the weekends."

"So?"

"We'll see," he said with quiet confidence, choosing his moment to pick up his pint. "Matter is to life as -"

"Life is to matter," said Kevin, completing Steve's favourite phrase. What it really meant and where he got it from nobody knew. Was mattering another way of saying finding love?

The two rarely looked at each other. They looked straight ahead or at the other patrons or at their pints, or they idly inspected the variety of beer mats on the table.

Kevin checked his watch.

"Easy. They'll be here," said Steve.

Pause.

"Watch it, Terry's spotted ya."

Kevin looked up to see the landlord coming over. He was staring straight at him with hard eyes. He stopped before them, not taking his eyes off Kevin, who could not look away and could not look him in the eye. To do that would be a challenge.

"Didn't see you come in."

"I was at the bar."

Terry nodded slowly.

"You didn't sneak in, then?"

He was pushing Kevin.

"Awh, come off it, Tell," he ventured a smile. A you-know-me smile. Had he overdone it?

Steve could not see the submission in Kevin's eyes.

The landlord wagged his finger at him.

"You just behave yourself."

"Yeah," promised Kevin, casting his eyes downward. No room for larking here.

Terry lingered for a moment and then left.

"Lucky," murmured Steve without moving his lips.

"Piece a cake," smiled Kevin.

"Oh, yeah, no sweat."

They'd almost finished their pints.

"How're getting on with that girl, er, what's her name? Thingamajig, er, Helen?"

"Oh, fine. Fine."

Pause.

"I saw her today," Kevin elaborated. "Pub lunch and a walk."

"Very nice."

"It was okay."

Kevin knew that Steve was not being funny. He was not like that. Kevin also knew that his own last remark would carry some weight.

"I know what you mean. I sometimes wonder why we bother," smiled Steve.

Kevin smiled, but felt himself sinking rapidly.

"It makes me wonder," he said, tilting the last of the brown liquid in his glass.

"Wonder what?" asked Steve, noting the gravity in Kevin's words.

"Why we bother. Why anything. Sometimes."

"Bloody hell," chuckled Steve, although not whole-heartedly. "You're not going to smash that glass and slit you wrists, are you?"

Kevin chuckled too.

"Ah, it's shit, I know," he resigned. Then, half-recovering, "What's that thing someone said to me." It had been Beryl. "Men are like toilets: either full of shit or occupied."

They smiled at this.

Then Steve said: "Sex is great, but it's nothing like the real thing."

There was another pause. And they realised that despite these quips the heaviness lingered.

"No, it's not like that," said Kevin. "Not that bad. But really, don't you sometimes get the feeling you're not really here?"

To his surprise Steve nodded. Maybe he did know

what he meant. It was too difficult to explain. It certainly wasn't a complete feeling of being outside oneself, like in a dream when you're both the participant and observer. No, it went deeper than that. In any case, he couldn't explain it.

Steve stood up, threw the remains of his pint down his throat and picking up Kevin's empty glass, asked "Same again?"

"Yeah," he replied, glad of his friend's understanding and wanting to come out of his declining state.

The pub was primarily frequented by rugby players. Terry played in a team. This ensured that the beer was good. A family atmosphere lingered amongst the hard-core patrons. Yet, it was not a clique. It was a friendly atmosphere.

Kevin knew a lot of the faces. For himself, he had no interest in rugby. If anything, the nearest thing was football. Even this was pursued with little more than casual interest. He did love boxing, though. That was the biz.

The hubbub of voices in the pub drowned the pop music that was being played. Occasionally, there'd be a darts tournament around the other side and trays of sandwiches would be offered to everyone. Then there'd be a promotional evening and some beverage would be offered at a considerable reduction. And so it went on. Never a dull moment.

It was just as Steve sat down that Tony, Ian and Chris came in.

After initial greetings, Tony remarked that he'd timed it well, pointing to the drinks on the table. He then asked his companions what their poison was and went to the bar.

"Bit late," remarked Kevin, as the two newcomers found stools and placed themselves on the other side of the table.

"I told Tony to pick me up at half-nine. We're not late at all," protested Chris. Then nodding at Ian. "Met 'im outside."

"Jeeez," exclaimed Steve. "You lot couldn't organise a piss-up in a brewery."

But Kevin's remark had been directed at Ian.

"Yeah, well, the phone rang as I got to the door. I had to answer it. A mate's trying to fix me up at his factory."

"How's tricks?" asked Chris, putting his jacket beside Steve.

"Survivin'," returned Steve.

"Heard you showed someone the way to the Royal last night, Kev?"

"I don't think I did him that much damage. Just something for him to think about."

"Didn't expect to see you in here," Chris went on, lighting up a cigarette.

Tony came up to the table, putting the three pints down and seating himself on the stool Ian had fetched for him.

"Cheers, Tone," said Chris, taking up his pint.

"Yeah, thanks mate," added Ian.

"Down yer necks, boys," he returned. Then to Kevin: "How was your head this morning?"

"Like shit."

He laughed. "Yeah."

"We're gettin' old," said Kevin.

"Speak for yourself," Steve put in.

"Is Smithy coming?" asked Ian.

"Yeah, I think so," answered Chris.

"What do you call a contented cannibal?" asked Ian.

"Heard it," said Kevin.

"Someone who's fed up with people," groaned Tony,

putting a cigarette between his lips.

"How about the penis and the foot?" Ian went on.

"Heard it," said Steve.

"Go on, I haven't," said Kevin.

All the time the group supped their pints. They were quite loud. But then the volume of noise in the pub was high.

"Have you heard it?" Ian asked Chris.

"No, I don't think so."

"I think I might have. I'm not sure," said Tony.

"Let's hear it," said Kevin.

"Okay." He paused to take a quick drink and ensure that he had their attention. "So the feet are complaining to the penis." It was then Ian looked about himself to check the people in the vicinity. He knew he was being loud. "It's all right for you. We're cooped up in the shoes all day. Hot and sweaty. In these smelly socks -"

"Know what you mean," remarked Steve.

"And we get walked on all day. Up and down stairs, along the streets. The whole weight of the body on us. It's a real strain. We -"

"I have heard it," said Tony.

"- sweat and strain. Life's no pleasure. Day in, day out -"

"Get on with it," said Chris. "Talk about stringing it out."

"Yeah," said Kevin. "I think we get the message Ian. They're pretty pissed off."

"Right." He takes another quick drink. "So the penis replies: you think you've got it bad. At least at the end of the day you get a good rest. He keeps me up half the night doing press-ups till I'm sick."

Kevin and Chris chuckled and Tony and Steve

smiled.

There were another couple of jokes and then Kevin got up to buy a round. Chris said he was skint and that it'd be better if they kept in their groups to buy the rounds. This was agreed and Kevin went to the bar to get Steve and himself more beer.

As the chap behind the bar pulled the pints, Kevin felt decidedly bloated. The sheer bulk of liquid on top of all that food filled him. He needed a good burp. True, mash was good stomach lining and he didn't feel any effects, but the quantity was another matter. He knew he would have to slow down.

As he manoeuvred through the crowd, a pint in each hand, he felt his eyes burning with the cigarette smoke. How he hated it. Oh yes, there was a time when he had smoked, but it had been vanquished by his thirst for fitness. Here, in the pub, you could get lung cancer from the atmosphere. Passive smoking, what a bummer.

He loathed the smarting of his eyes and his bloated feeling. And for an instant, he wondered what he was doing.

Wouldn't it be nice just to stay in with a woman? Yes, at this moment he wanted that. A quiet night in. It appealed. He'd had a lot of that with Sandra. At first it had been stifling, and although he had enjoyed its security, he had fought it. Slowly, he and his world had come to accept it. His world adapted. He had moaned and grumbled about freedom and he had flirted when he had been away from her and out with the lads. Now she was gone. At first he had felt terribly lonely. Something was missing. The guts of him had been torn out. But slowly his world had changed. Back to the moaning. Hunting again. Sniffing around. Never satisfied.

Where was she now? He'd had a letter some nine

months ago, but that was the last.

"Cheers, Kev," said Steve, taking his pint.

"Seen that blonde over there?" asked Tony quietly to Kevin, stubbing out his cigarette.

"Yeah," replied Kevin, having seated himself and putting his pint to his lips. However, he took another look at her. She was gorgeous. "She's with that pleb over there."

"What? The smoothie with the tash?"

"Yep."

"What a waste of good talent."

Kevin looked to the others and realised that they were talking about football. Tony didn't care for sport or any form of physical exertion for that matter. He liked beer and women.

The football conversation was a banal argument about the worth of a certain player. Kevin ignored them.

"What did you do today?" asked Tony.

"Nothing much. Went for a lunchtime drink." He hadn't wanted to tell him this, but he hadn't wanted to lie either.

"With that architect, no doubt."

"Yeah."

"Poked her yet?"

"None of your business."

"You should have brought her along."

"What? To meet you animals? You've got to be joking."

"I've met her once."

"That was enough."

Kevin remembered it well. His own embarrassment had made the three of them quite awkward. Tony had caught them in town on their way to the pictures for the evening.

"Come on, Kev."

"Your rudeness embarrassed her."

"Come off it. She was smiling. As I remember it, it was you who was embarrassed."

"I wasn't. And she was being polite."

"Naw. I bet she knows a few dirty jokes herself."

Kevin decided that the conversation was getting out of hand and quite silly to boot.

"Pah, maybe."

Pause.

"I don't know what you're getting so uppity about. Okay, so we're not good enough for her."

Kevin knew that Tony was a hair's breadth from bringing the others in on the conversation. Then it really would get silly.

"Drop it, Tone."

They supped their pints.

"I'll bring her along when I'm good an' ready."

"She's got you by the balls, hasn't she?"

Box clever, thought Kevin. Let the baby win. Side with him.

"It's just that I'm not sure where I stand. We're not going out yet and I'm not sure that I want to."

Half truths.

Would this sincerity win the big oaf over?

"You'd better knuckle down, mate," he advised, lighting another cigarette. "She's better than fuckin' a pig, although she's not my cup of tea. I'd watch it if I were you, she looks like a clever one. Have you running circles round yourself."

Sod him, Kevin thought. One day he'd smash him. He only tolerated the big lug because he was Chris's friend.

"Three F's, that's what I say. Find 'em. Fuck 'em.

Forget 'em."

Kevin smiled and took a gulp from his pint. If you had shit for brains you'd be dangerous, Tone. Yeah, you can be the wise one for now, but one day I'll belt you.

Strangely, Kevin felt that Tony liked him. Perhaps admired him. And that he was trying to impress him, to befriend him. The stupid fool was going about it all the wrong way. He just had no idea.

"Where's Smithy?" asked Tony of the group.

Ian made a circle with his right hand index finger and thumb and moved it over his nose.

"Fuck nose," translated Steve.

"He's a waste of space," said Chris.

"A large space, at that," added Steve.

"My round kids," said Ian. "Same again?" he asked Chris and Tony.

When he had gone, Steve asked: "What's wrong with him? He seems a bit hyper, as if he's hiding something."

"Yeah, he's lower than a snake's arse in the grass," remarked Tony.

"His Mum's not well," said Kevin.

"Oh yeah, I remember him mentioning it now," said Chris.

"What's wrong with her?" enquired Steve.

"I think they've diagnosed pleurisy."

Kevin nodded in agreement.

A silence fell upon the group.

Kevin checked his drinking progress with that of Steve. Damn, he was drinking like a fish.

"That Debbie's something else," commented Chris, taking out another cigarette. He called all blondes Debbie. Debbie Harry.

"Yeah, we clocked that earlier," said Tony.

112

"It makes me laugh," began Steve. "We spend the first nine months trying to get out and then the rest of our lives trying to get back in!"

They chuckled.

When Ian returned more jokes were passed around and they went on to talk about Kevin's fight. After this they discussed the latest developments in the miners' dispute. During this time Steve bought another round and went to the loo.

"It's all gone political," stated Chris.

Kevin nodded. "Yep, and who gets hurt? The miners and the pigs. Poor sods."

"It's bleedin' Thatcher," accused Tony.

"Scargill's made a mess of the whole thing," said Chris.

"That's the media, mate," said Tony. "They've ripped him to bits."

"He's made mistakes," said Kevin.

"If you ask me," began Ian, "the whole country's going to pot."

"Too right," agreed Steve, raising his pint.

"It's bleedin' Thatcher," grumbled Ian.

"Well, they say it's truly an ill wind that blows nobody any good," said Chris. "And if you take a look at my brother, you'll see what I mean. He's what Thatcher's about. His electrical wholesaling business is going a bomb."

"That may be," said Ian. "But she won't get my vote."

"It'll take another Falklands for them to win again," said Steve.

"There's talk of getting rid of the rates," began Tony. "They're going to try it out in Scotland."

"What?" asked Kevin.

"I don't rightly know. A sort of tax per person instead

of household."

"Ah, it'll never see the light of day."

"The whole thing's a disaster," said Ian. "No job, no future. It's the pits."

"Bugger it all me-hearties," said Tony, taking a good gulp from his sleever. "This is what it's all about," he said pointing to his pint.

"An' bein' with y'mates," said Ian, looking more cheerful.

"An' gettin' yer hole," Tony added.

They all laughed.

Kevin thought that they were right. Ordinarily, he didn't agree with Tony, but at this moment in time he felt he was right. Sod the country.

"Yeah, having a laugh with y'mates," said Kevin.

"Oh yeah. I haven't had so much fun since I had beri-beri," said Chris.

"Laugh? I almost shat!" said Steve.

They were all quite loud. Almost shouting. The place was packed. All the seats were taken and most of the standing room was occupied with very little room to move about.

The conversation moved on to recent films and they discussed what they had seen and what they'd like to see. Kevin bought the drinks and Chris joined him to buy his own round.

By now Kevin was struggling. This was his fifth pint and it was having an effect. At this rate he felt he would have to move over to shorts. He couldn't take the volume tonight. But he hated going on to shorts. It was evil. He would rapidly decline and the following day his head and stomach would be in agony.

He set down the drinks and then went for a slash. On

his return he asked: "Seen the new Durex machine?"

"Yeah," said Tony. The others nodded or shook their heads.

"Pull knob to return coins," said Kevin.

They laughed.

"I saw one at Wolverhampton station," said Chris.

"Wolverhampton!" exclaimed Steve.

"There was a match."

"Don't tell me," began Ian. "It said: this is the worst tasting bubble-gum I've ever had."

"No. On the side somebody had scratched: buy one and stop one, buy two and be one step ahead, buy three and fuck all the virgins in Wolverhampton."

They laughed.

Shortly after this Smithy appeared at the door.

Steve was the first to see him through the crowd.

"Smithy," he called.

"Here he comes," said Tony. "Our man in Havana. The FBI, fat, bald and ignorant."

They smiled.

"Hiya," Smithy greeted, when he had reached their table.

"Look what the cat dragged in," said Chris.

"What time do you call this?" asked Ian.

"Ha! Pot calling the kettle black," attacked Kevin.

At the same time Smithy replied: "'bout twenty past ten."

"You're a waste of space," said Chris.

"Yeah, yeah. Let me get a drink."

"Mine's a pint," said Tony.

"Sod off," returned Smithy, noting their full pints. He went off to the bar.

"He's putting on some weight," commented Steve.

"There was a time when he was built like a brick shit-house," said Chris.

"Aye. That's what a wife does for yer," said Tony, reaching for the matches to light up.

"Hey, lay off about that," warned Chris, getting up to go to the loo. "I told you it's not going so well."

A silence fell upon the group for a moment and Kevin looked again to the entrance. Behind Smithy he had noticed a couple. He searched them out and could just catch glimpses of them at the bar. There was something about them that had caught his attention. What was it? He inspected them. No, it wasn't physical, it was something more. Something they represented, or seemed to represent. Then he had it.

They were of Helen's ilk. Calm. Their disposition showed no challenge, no anger, no hidden frustration. Maybe they were going out, maybe they were married. It did not matter.

The lads had started up again, talking this time about a local murder.

Kevin's eyes smarted with the smoke as he continued to spy the couple.

He did not know what he was feeling, but evidently his expression said something, for Smithy remarked on it when he returned.

"Hey, snap out of it, Kev," he said. "You look positively manic," he smiled.

"Ah, I was miles away."

"Anyone would've thought you were a space-case," he said squatting at the table.

"Huh." Kevin did not have a reply.

"Here, I can move along a bit," said Steve, picking up Chris's jacket and putting it beside the table next to Chris, who, in turn, adjusted its position.

"You won't find enough room for him," said Tony.

"Up yours!"

But they did find enough room for him on the bench.

"This is cosy," said Kevin, wedged between Steve and Smithy.

The others resumed their conversation.

Tony went to the loo.

"You okay then, Kev?" asked Smithy.

"Yeah, fine. How's yourself?"

"Middlin'." He supped his pint. "Spot of the old self-indulgence just now, was it?"

Self-indulgence. There was a good phrase, thought Kevin.

"Yeah," he replied.

The two of them joined the main conversation. It was blatantly obvious that Smithy wanted to be one of the lads. But they were all well on their way to getting pissed and he was sober.

Smithy drank as quickly as he could and when he had finished it was time for Steve's round.

Kevin said he'd have the same again. He had found his second breath.

"Good man," praised Steve, slightly unsteady on his feet. "You might as well come in with us, Smithy."

"Wouldn't say no."

"I'd watch that," said Kevin, noting his rapid consumption and patting Smithy on the belly.

"You're not doing so bad yourself. When's it due?"

"That's just my shirt."

"You know Smithy," began Chris, "you're the only bloke in the pub who's sitting next to everybody."

"Ha, bloody ha."

And they all laughed.

Kevin glanced about and noticed that no other table seemed to be having as much fun as them. Yes, this was what it was all about. Having a laugh. Okay, they were laughing like children, but what better way to laugh?

Steve returned and Smithy, still trying to be part of the group, although in reality, he had been accepted long ago by each and every one of them, took centre stage.

"Did you hear about Jim last night?" he asked.

They all replied that they had not. Chris hadn't seen him for about three weeks. Ian said he'd seen him in town a couple of days ago and had invited him along tonight.

"You're not likely to see him for a while."

"Why?" asked Ian.

"Well lads," he began, taking a quick sip of his beer. "He got absolutely arse-holed last night."

"Didn't we all," said Tony.

"No, wait for it. This is brilliant. Brian told me over the phone this morning. I didn't believe it myself -"

"Don't tell me," interrupted Tony. "He threw up over a car again -"

"And then pissed it off!" ended Chris.

"Yeah, tidy bastard," said Tony.

There were chuckles.

"What happened?" asked Ian of Smithy.

"Apparently he picks up a girl -"

"Jeez, he has more success when he's blotto than I do when I'm sober," remarked Steve.

"Understandable," said Tony.

"Bog off!"

"Let him tell it," said Ian, frustratedly.

"She's the type of girl you wouldn't spit on if she were on fire," said Smithy.

"A real grimmie," put in Chris.

"A two paper bag job," said Kevin, enjoying the sport of postponing the story.

"Two?" queried Steve.

"Yeah, one of her head like normal and one over yours."

"Over yours?"

"Yeah, just in case hers comes off!"

They all laughed.

"And she was covered in small round welts," said Tony. He paused and then added: "From where the barge pole had been hitting her."

"To the grimmies of the world!" toasted Chris.

And they all raised their glasses.

"As I said, he was really pissed." Smithy took another gulp of beer to ensure that they were back with him. "He gets her back to his flat and he's on top of her, doing the business and -"

"He's got syphilis," Chris guessed, giving his cigarette a last pull.

"No, no. Will you give us a chance?"

"Bugger me," began Ian.

"Not while there're dogs on the street," said Kevin.

"Ha, ha," returned Ian. "Look I'm bursting for a piss, hold off your story till I get back."

"No. Wait," said Smithy.

"Get on with it then."

"It's not my fault."

"All right, everyone shut up. Let him get on with his bleedin' story."

Just then Tony leant over and with the flat of his hand pushed in Ian's stomach.

Ian pushed him off.

"Bastard."

The effect was to increase his urge to urinate. Tony laughed and the others smiled.

"He's on top of her -" Smithy began.

"Cor blimey, somebody's got bad guts," said Kevin.

"Paaww, yeah. Somebody's really dropped one," agreed Steve.

"Will we ever hear this story?" asked Ian.

"Urggh," added Tony, "the silent ones are the worst."

But nobody owned up.

"He's on top of her, see," Smithy resumed. "And he's just finished givin' it some, when he throws up -"

"Shit a brick!" exclaimed Ian, desperately trying to forget his physical needs.

"Over the side of the bed, right?" asked Chris.

"No. Over her."

"Fuck a pig!" exclaimed Tony.

"Bloody hell," said Kevin.

"Jeeeeez," said Steve.

They were all laughing and looking at each other with distasteful, humorous faces.

"A pavement pizza in bed is bad enough," said Ian, "but over someone else -"

"At least he got 'is 'ole first," said Tony.

Before the laughter took a firm hold Smithy went on loudly.

"There's more. I haven't got to the punch-line, yet." Once again he gulped a mouthful of beer. Then he began again enthusiastically. "He wakes up this morning and she's gone -"

"Wait a minute. What happened after he gave her the multi-coloured yawn?" asked Steve, suspiciously.

"I don't know. Brian thinks he couldn't remember.

She probably cleaned up a bit. I don't know. I think all Jim remembers is the up-chuck."

"Arrgh," remarked Chris.

More ripples of laughter.

Smithy drank his beer until they'd simmered down.

"Go on Smithy," said Ian.

"He wakes up and he's pretty pleased, to say the least, that she's gone. The smell was pretty bad, though." He paused again, this time to finish his pint and see through further chuckles. "Then he becomes aware of something on his chest. He lifts up the sheets to find this whopping turd sitting on him."

At this the group was thrown into fits of hysteria.

"You're joking?" questioned Tony. "It's got to be a joke."

"No. You ask Jim when you next see him."

"Brill," exclaimed Kevin.

"Talk about faux pas," said Smithy.

And the laughter continued.

"Cor, I haven't laughed so much since granny caught her tit in the mangle!" said Chris, coining his standard phrase.

"Talk about don't get mad, get even," said Steve. "It wasn't steaming, was it?"

"I think I'm going to wet myself," said Ian, rising from the table, bent over in agony and rushing off.

This injected the group with further peals of laughter.

"I think I'm going to pee in me pants, too," said Chris, tears running down his face.

How loud and raucous they were. No matter, they were having fun.

Kevin knew that it probably wasn't whopping either. But it'd become a whopping, steaming thing over time.

"My stomach hurts," grinned Kevin, getting up to buy the next round.

"Pint?" he asked.

"Cheers," replied Smithy, handing Kevin his sleever.

"Good man," acknowledged Steve.

When Kevin returned, fighting his way through the crowd, he found that they were again talking about his fight. Smithy knew nothing of it, but Kevin played it down, wanting to return to the humour.

Another pint was had before closing time. The humour continued, but not as raucously; everyone trying a little too hard. They laughed at silly things, because they were drunk.

They were some of the last to leave.

At one point Terry had come to them and asked what the joke was. Of course, no one was willing to tell him, for the whole pub would be listening. As it was they felt isolated, although people in the immediate vicinity could have heard the story. In any case, what they had been laughing at when he had interrupted them had not been terribly funny. This had made them laugh all the more.

They spilled out into the night, waiting near the entrance for those who had gone to the loo.

Tony suggested going back to his place. He had some gin and vodka.

Smithy excused himself and they let him go. Steve, Ian and Chris said they would join him, but Kevin wanted to get away. He was absolutely wrecked. In addition, he was starving.

"Come on Kev, join us," said Steve.

"Why? Are you falling apart?" he returned.

"Come on, let's get on. It's freezing out here. Make up your mind," said Chris.

"Naw, I'm feeling knackered."

"No stamina," accused Steve.

"Are you driving?" Kevin asked.

"You've got to be joking," said Tony.

"No, I really must get home."

"You'll come if I drive?"

"No. Forget it, really. I'm going to crash."

"Get yer beauty sleep."

"Something like that."

"You need it."

Kevin smiled. With that they let him go.

The temptation had been great. But he'd have regretted it in the morning. He knew.

Kevin had turned from them after telling them he'd phone during the week. Perhaps they'd go to the club on Thursday?

The night was damp, the sky cloudless and the wind sharp, sometimes crisp. A large moon made the scene a smoky grey against the brittle, inky black sky peppered with winking stars.

He watched his training shoes appear alternately below him. The street was deserted. More hushed than before. If that were possible. But he didn't care. He felt isolated from it all and just wanted to get back.

As he walked, at an unnaturally brisk pace, he brought a hand to an ear. Ice cold. At school they'd sneaked up on unsuspecting kids and vigorously rubbed their ears. Kevin had had it done to himself. How sore it made them!

"He lifts up the sheets to find this great turd sitting on him!"

Kevin's smile was twisted by the cold.

The roads were quiet. He could have been the only person in the whole wide world. He smiled when he heard the introductory music to the Twilight Zone.

"You look at my woman again I'll put you in an oxygen tent!"

"Yeah, you and whose fuckin' army?" Kevin murmured, without moving his lips.

And his shoes appeared below him as he urged them on. Left, right. Left, right.

He looked up and saw the corner where he'd been attacked. Two of them had laid into him. He hadn't had a chance. All he remembered were the blows and pain, the sound of his drunk's pocket spilling onto the pavement and shadows and the salty taste of blood in his mouth. Then they were picking up the coins. And he had closed his eyes to it all. Did he cry? Then the brightness of the hospital.

Once again, he was pissed and an ideal target. Shit, he would run. He'd run like the wind. He only had a fiver. Last time he'd had close on twenty quid. Bastards. Left, right. Left, right. They'd done him in good and proper.

He tensed himself as he passed the alley. Keep going. Left, right. Left, right.

Then he was at the bottom of the hill. He couldn't remember crossing the road. Ah well, up the hill.

Left, right. Left, right.

It was on such a drunken night that he'd stolen the dustbin from the bottom of the hill. Trouble was, it had been full! It was raining too. Anyhow, he carried it away. What a sot.

He recalled that he'd missed his exercise that day, and in his anxiety to get in out of the cold, he decided to run up the hill. Yes, all the way to his door. He'd run off the beer.

With his hands out of his pockets, one hand gripping the umbrella, he ran up the hill. Left, right, left, right, left, right.

He began to count his steps to spur himself on, but he lost count in the mid-two hundreds and settled down to a faltering jog as he neared his flat.

When he pushed the key into the door he thought of visiting Beryl.

"Two times," she gasped. "That's never happened before."

But he dismissed this on grounds that it was early for a Saturday night and she would more than likely be out. He'd had a good time. Why spoil it? No, leave her alone. Don't be pathetic.

The phrase 'madonnas and whores' came to mind and he wondered why it was so in his life. Ah, but Sandra...

In the flat he tossed down his jacket and umbrella, and noisily set about making himself a cheese on toast.

On with the kettle.

He was angered by the pile of dishes in the bowl.

"Ah, sod off!" he said to them. Then he chuckled.

Clumsily, he cut the cheese and made himself a coffee.

"Don't you ever get the feeling you're not really here?"

When everything was done he carried it off to the lounge. There he slumped on the sofa, after putting on the television.

"It's not a film. There needn't be a happy ending. Or a proper ending."

He stared wearily at the picture for a time, the cheese on toast on a plate in his lap. He greedily attacked the food as if he'd never eaten.

After this vicious consumption, placing the plate beside him, he picked up his mug of coffee and gently blowing over its surface he sipped it. But it was far too hot and scalded the insides of his mouth.

"Shit," he exclaimed.

There was some kind of debate on the television. Some nuclear thing. A young man, probably a conservative, asked a question. Kevin did not hear it. The bloke reminded him of the couple in the pub. He was probably screwing her right now! No different to him. Or maybe they were having a debate? He smiled at this.

Then he thought of Helen and her 'sexual barrier'.

"We'll just be friends."

What was he doing? It was impossible. Why was he wasting his time?

And he saw her as a rabbit and himself as a wolf. Well, that said it all. Luckily she'd not picked up on it. Or had she? Shit. How could he be such a div?

"Who needs it?" he said to himself. It's not that important. Yeah, fuck it.

"Oh, shut up," he said and switched off the television. He then sat and stared at the blank screen.

Yes, who needs it? And all the so-called literature. The challenge was to find the meaning. Even no meaning was a meaning. He smiled again. Wandering nobodies, wandering nowhere.

He got up, teetered for a moment, the mug still in his hand, and went to the table.

Kevin stared down at the pad for a long while. Slowly something suggested itself to him and he sat down.

His thoughts remained higgledy-piggledy. So he sipped his coffee. His mind was a hive of activity as he picked up the pen. But it was all chaos. And anger pulled down his brow. Then something set and his lips drew thin over his clenched teeth. He flipped over the top page from 'Dear Aunty, Sorry for not writing sooner. There's no excuses.' and a blank sheet stared back at him.

He hesitated.

Then, as if possessed, he wrote furiously; pausing only twice, and adding the title at the end as he'd been taught at school. His writing was erratic, illegible in places, full of mistakes and crossings-out.

What the Fuck

After all this you realise nothing can touch you unless you let it. Pregnancy, VD, death, what the fuck. You let it get to you if you want it to. Everyone needs a little self-indulgence, a little self-pity, but it can become addictive. Too much is bad for you. So have a laugh. Have a little tipple. Give y'self a little. If it can't be love, a substitute is not always so bad. Loosen up. Lighten up.

Drive that car with fluid aggression. What the fuck. Take that girl who's pissed out of her brain. What the fuck. Wank yourself silly. Drink yourself legless. Punch that bag. Run that race. Lift that weight. Hurt that pain. Knacker yourself. What the fuck. Burn that energy. Be bright and brilliant for a moment. Shine for that second, brighter than anything in the Universe.

And when you're spent and wasted. Wondering, wondering. What the fuck.

We're all just scratching the mountain. Crawling our way up. Looking for a niche. Looking for a hole in which to crawl. And when we're there? Huh, what the fuck.

And then there's this writing. Itself a form of intellectual (really?) wanking. But this is what people like. Oh, they love Satre and Hamsun. They love this kind of guttural sincerity. "Just how can they live their lives feeling, believing, what they do? What makes them tick?" The reader wonders. You really want to know? It's self-indulgence. Crawling up their arses and getting paid for it. Ha. Shove it, man. Shove it.

You want meaninglessness? I say, what the fuck. Because great if you've got meaning, tough if you haven't, but in the end you sit back and it all ends with a smile: What the fuck.

Kevin lurched to his feet and left the room taking his coffee with him. He got a pint of water, clattering about with the dishes in the bowl, in a sleever he'd stolen from some pub a long time back. Then he went to the bedroom, switching the lights out behind him and closing the door.

(Look out for the sequel "Bottle" which continues Kevin's story.)

www.ingramcontent.com/pod-product-compliance
Lightning Source LLC
Chambersburg PA
CBHW031608260626
47154CB00020B/1708